THE LOST TESTAMENT OF JUDAS ISCARIOT

Brandon Originals

The Lost Testament
of Judas Iscariot

Michael Dickinson

BRANDON

First published in 1994 by
Brandon Book Publishers Ltd,
Dingle, Co. Kerry, Ireland

All quotations from the Bible are from the Authorised
(King James) Version.

This book is published with the financial assistance of
the Arts Council/An Chomhairle Ealaíon, Ireland.

British Library Cataloguing in Publication Data is
available for this book.

ISBN 0 86322 178 5

Front cover illustration: *Christ of St John of the Cross*
by Salvador Dali, reproduced by permission of Glasgow
Museums: The St Mungo Museum of Religious Life &
Art.

Cover design: The Graphiconies, Dublin
Typesetting: Koinonia Ltd, Bury
Printed by ColourBooks Ltd, Dublin

The Son of man goeth as it is written of him: but woe unto that man by whom the Son of man is betrayed! it had been good for that man if he had not been born.

Matthew 26:24

Now this man purchased a field with the reward of iniquity; and falling headlong, he burst asunder in the midst, and all his bowels gushed out.

Acts 1:18

Preface

The document you are about to read was passed on to me by an unnamed contact who works in the Vatican. He claims it to be the translation of a manuscript which has been kept there under conditions of strict secrecy for several centuries.

It is not for me to say whether the document is authentic or not – I leave you to make your own decision. Read it with an open mind.

Apart from changing a few archaic words and phrases to make it more understandable to a modern reader, I have interfered with the script as little as possible.

Michael Dickinson
Istanbul 1994

*And he cast down the pieces of silver in the temple,
and departed, and went and hanged himself.*

Matthew 27:5

The fat black spider is busy in her web in the corner of the ceiling, leisurely gathering and cocooning the unwary moths attracted in from the dark outside. They struggle and flutter in vain for freedom. Fate has lured them here to their doom. Fate – and the light of my irresistibly treacherous lamp.

I sit crouched, cross-legged on the slab as I write. The pits and grooves of the hewn rock around me undulate with shadows, creating shapes and faces as the wavering flame flickers upon them, parading whole scenes from my life. Thank God Martha has allowed me the means to tear my eyes away from the horrors they unfold, with this papyrus,

9

stylus and ink. Without them, I believe I could easily become trapped within memories and slide into insanity. My shadow looms huge on the wall behind me, like some patient evil djinn waiting for me to finish my scribbling and come away with him to Hell.

It is so silent that I sometimes believe I have become deaf. Then when I concentrate on listening hard, I hear the blood throbbing in my temples, the malignant whine of a mosquito honing in on that blood and the slap of my hand against my face as I thwart it. Occasionally I hear a distant dog howling about the moon or something, and echoing howls, faint and far away, answer him almost instantly. Dogs, at least, understand each other.

The thought comes to me that if we could learn their language there would be no more need for letters or messengers. One would simply dictate the message to a cur, and it would be howled from one to another throughout the country in less than an hour.

But even if it were possible, it would, of course, be considered politically dangerous, and suppressed. Apart from that, if everybody used the dog-system to communicate, no one would be able to hear a thing. There would such be a continual blare of yelps, yips, growls and howls, all so mixed up together, that nothing would be decipherable. Perhaps it's better left alone. But whatever messages they are passing on tonight, their lonely howls strike a corresponding chord in my own loneliness which sends a shiver down my spine despite the heat. It is a very humid night, not a breath of air stirring. Sweat streams down from my forehead, making my beard a mass of wet coils. My shirt sticks to my back. Although I am confined here in the tomb, the gap usually allows an occasional waft of breeze to enter and cool me. Not tonight. The air is like thick, warm blood. The stars visible through the gap hang motionless in a stagnant, black sea of sky.

It's after midnight. Could I not take a walk out among the olive-trees and oleanders, the perfume of whose blossoms reach me here, blending with the oily smoke of the lamp? A walk would refresh me, invigorate me, restore my faith in myself. No. Nothing could do that. Not anymore.

And I couldn't risk it. Admittedly, everyone is asleep at this hour. But perhaps out there in the dark, curled up under a tree, might be a sleeping dog which would awake and speak in the language that human beings do understand. Not the undecipherable lonely howl, but the strident, snarling warning that arouses households. A stranger abroad! A prowler in the vicinity! And out they would come with lamps and cudgels to find me cornered, fending off the savage brute. Imagine the surprise as they hold up their lanterns to shine in my face as I vainly try to shield it with my hands.

"You! Judas! What are you doing here? We thought you were dead! Why aren't you dead? After what you did you ought to be dead!" And they advance on me with their heavy sticks, showering me with stones and spittle, screaming curses and accusations. "Spy! Traitor! Murderer!" No. I won't take a walk tonight. Or any other night. I am safe here in the tomb.

Martha is the only one who knows I am still alive. She

11

tells me people believe I committed suicide out of shame for what I had done. Hanged myself on a tree in some grove, and am rotting there, unburied and unwept. Sometimes I think that is what I should have done instead of running grovelling here to her, pleading with her to hide me.

She could not hide her bitterness and disgust. But I had no doubt that she would take me in. She is an angel, and it shouldn't have been necessary for me to remind her to do unto others as she would have them do unto her, but her icy silence forced me to in desperation. She looked at me in horrified disbelief. I had the nerve to say such a thing after what I had done! Like everybody else, she believes that I am the filthy traitor, lower than the lowest scum, the damned murdering betrayer of the Master. And she must continue to believe it. I cannot tell her the truth. I can tell no one. To protect the Master's reputation, I must remain mute and accept the role of villain.

It was Martha who suggested the tomb. The house would have been too dangerous. I would have been seen by a servant and the news would have spread. The tomb was the perfect solution. Far down at the end of the garden, out of sight of the house and olive-press, sheltered by the grove and conveniently empty after the resurrection of Lazarus. Could he not at least remember that and forgive me for what I did? O Master! My Master! Can you not understand that all was for your sake?

And so here I live like a beast within my lair. The stone is pushed aside just enough for a man to squeeze in or out. Martha, being small, enters easily when she comes at night with my supper. Our eyes rarely meet. Everything she does is performed briskly and in silence. She places the food and flagon on the slab and takes the covered pot in the corner, replacing it with a clean one. At first I was terribly ashamed, apologising for the stench and the degradation I was causing her, but she replied that it was nothing to the filth I had performed in Jerusalem. I understood what she meant, and could not reply.

How long have I been here? Days and nights stretch out like a long, heavy chain. Weeks. Perhaps even months. I try to sleep during the days, but I often wake abruptly from a vision of the Master's frowning face, and his stern, cold words like swords in my heart – "I will never forgive you." Than I cry and pray to God, for I know that He forgives me. But that is not enough. It is the Master's love and forgiveness I crave. I am nothing without it.

At night the silence is unbearable. It's not so bad during the day. I can hear the grinding of the oil-press and the occasional laughter of the workers. How beautiful the sound of laughter is! And yet how painful at the same time. For I know that I will never laugh again.

Once, Martha brought some curious visitors down to look at the tomb, and I lay inside, rigid, hardly daring to breath, as they stood outside marvelling, while she, in her flat, matter-of-fact voice, related the story of her brother's resurrection. How he had fallen ill and the Master had been sent for, but before his arrival Lazarus had died, been anointed and entombed. Three days later the Master had arrived while they were still mourning, ordered the covering stone to be removed, and called Lazarus to return to life. Out he had come as though he had never been dead! Yes indeed, it had been a true miracle! Praise be to God!

I knew that Martha was aware that I was listening to her commentary from inside and could detect the cynicism in her tone, but she could not be aware of how proud of her I was. She is a true disciple and would never betray that secret. Sometimes I feel I could almost trust her with the rest. She would love me again. Twice as much for what I did. She would worship me as a hero. But it is impossible. Nobody must ever know. Ever.

Martha lives alone now. The news of his resurrection brought many visitors down from Jerusalem to inspect the miraculous Lazarus. One of them was a rich widow who offered herself in marriage, and he accepted her. He now lives in her mansion in the city, raking in the money from her inherited spice business. Mary has disappeared. Martha says she went insane after the crucifixion and claimed that the Master had appeared to her. She left home to find him and follow him. Oh that I could do the same! I would gladly die for just one last glimpse!

But sometimes my well of sorrow bubbles up with anger and indignation at the way I have been treated. Had it not been for me our whole cause, our whole struggle, would have come to nought. But what thanks did I receive? Anger. Hateful words. Accusations. And banishment from his sight forever. He would be King even now if he had shown himself. How the news would have spread! He would have been accepted as the Messiah by millions. Instead, he has disappeared to God knows where, leaving the mission unfulfilled. What was the point of it all? It could have culminated in the ultimate glory if he had listened to me.

I must try to sleep now and quell these sinful and rebellious thoughts. I still love you, Master. Nothing will change that. You have done as you thought best. But I cannot help but wish... If only...

Unbelievable news! Peter and the brothers are back preaching in Jerusalem! Martha brought me the tidings when she came with my food tonight. After the incident in the Garden of Gethsemane they fled the city and returned to Galilee, fearing for their lives, but a few days later the Master appeared to them while they were fishing. He talked with them and showed them the wounds in his hands. He told Peter to round up the others and return to Jerusalem, preach the gospel, spread the news of his resurrection, baptise and win new converts. He himself was going away for a time, but he would return soon and expected to find a rich harvest from their labours. Then he departed, warning them not to follow or try to find him.

He has done it! The mission has begun again! And although I can no longer take part in it myself, my pain and sorrow has partly been assuaged by the news.

Peter visited Martha this afternoon to give her the information. When she came to me tonight, her voice shook with incredulity. Peter had also spoken to Mary shortly after the Master had left them. She had appeared on the shore with a small bundle, asking which way he had gone. Peter had shown her, but warned that the Master had forbidden anybody to follow him. Mary said she knew, but that she could not help herself. She was prepared to suffer his rejection if she could only keep him in sight, and hoped that a day might come when he would need and accept her. Then, bidding him farewell, she had hurried off in the direction of the Master.

Peter says the brothers are filled with a stronger zeal than before. They preach tirelessly and are not afraid. Their witness of the Master has given them new spirit.

Peter preaches with them. Leads them. Proclaims his resurrection. And yet he knows. Oh what great faith! What devotion! To preach a lie for the love of the Master! May God bless him and protect him in his endeavours!

Peter is the only one who knows that I am not a traitor. He knows, but he does not fully understand. He was puzzled by what happened that night. Could I not share the secret with him and die uncursed by at least one good man? He would not lose faith. Even I, who know the full truth, have not.

Yes. I will relate the whole story to Peter. Confess it all, and let him judge me saint or sinner. I will write it down, and he, and only he, will read what I have written. Then the manuscript must be destroyed and the secret will be ours. I am certain that he would never reveal it, even with the threat of crucifixion.

And so, salutations to you my beloved brother Peter! Read my story, and things that puzzled you before will become clear. I beseech you that if and when the Master returns you will beg forgiveness for me for all that I did. Kiss him for me. Give him the expected kiss that I gave to another....

Every Kingdom divided against itself is brought to desolation; and every city or house divided against itself shall not stand...

Matthew 12:25

First I should tell you a little about myself. We lived and worked together, but we did not really know each other as individuals, or what brought us to devote our lives to the Master. Our identities did not matter. It was his message which we carried that was of prime importance.

I was born in Kerioth, in Judea. My mother died giving birth to me. My father was a potter. I don't remember him, for when I was only two years old he married a widow with children of her own, and I was sent to live with my Uncle Bartholomew and his family in Bethany. He was a fairly wealthy wine merchant, and we led a comfortable existence.

As a boy, I was so proud of my name. Judas! My grandfather had chosen it for me. I would sit silently at his knee and listen enthralled when he related the story of my namesake, Judas the Galilean, who had gathered an army of followers and risen against the Romans, to drive them out of our country. I never tired of hearing the story, and was awed by the fact that my grandfather, though a baby at the time, had been alive in those days. He swore that had he been older, he would have joined with Judas in his attempt to liberate the land.

My best friend Lazarus and I became obsessed with the tale, and enthused our other playmates likewise. Our favourite game become "Zealots versus Romans", which we played every day in the dusty backstreets. My heart would swell with pride whenever I was chosen to play the part of Judas, and my voice trembled with real passion as I rallied my followers.

"Our only duty is to God! We are free! Only through discontent, only through action, can the Messiah, the promised liberator, be found!"

And then we would fight tirelessly with our little wooden swords. Passing adults smiled or frowned at our antics, little realising that their liberty, their freedom, their very country depended upon the outcome of our battle.

But however hard we fought, we already knew the result, and that we were powerless to change the course of history. Our game stuck ruthlessly to the tragic facts of the story. The boy playing the part of the Roman commander, Varus, would always win the battle, and my little gang of four or five would be hung up on makeshift crosses to represent the two thousand rebels who had been truly crucified, while I, Judas, escaped to Lebanon. There was brief hope and elation while a fresh campaign was planned there, but the game would always end as it did in life, with the capture of Judas and his own crucifixion in Rome. Afterwards, we would part soberly and make our ways home, our thoughts a mixture of depression and hope. The Roman yoke must be thrown from our necks some day. Then, and only then, could the glorious reign of the Messiah begin.

As I grew older, like other children, I ceased to play such games. There was school, the memorising of the Torah, the taking on of responsibilities.

Time passed. Grandfather died. School finished. My uncle took me as a partner in his small but flourishing wine business. I became an adult. But like many adults my ideals remained those of my childhood, more intense though less revealed as I became aware of the dangers of carelessly showing my inner feelings to others.

I was not content with mere silent grudging acceptance of the Occupation, like my uncle and his family, or our religious leaders, who seemed to fawn on the Romans like pet dogs. There had to be something we could do to gain our freedom. My heart would burn with impotent rage whenever a garrison of Roman soldiers tramped through our village, raising the dust, or when I had to accompany my uncle to the tax collector to pay our debt to Caesar. Everywhere I could see the poverty and subjection of my people, while the conquerors lived off the fat of the land.

Sometimes, as I lay out on our flat roof under the stars on warm summer nights, I would become intoxicated by wild, bitter dreams. I would become a Zealot! I would take up arms like the Judas before me and drive the Roman dogs yelping into the sea! What had I to lose but my life? But then I would shudder, despite the sticky warmth of the night. I remembered the outcome of my grandfather's tale, and saw myself groaning and wracked in the agony of the slow and terrible death of the cross. A matter of callous routine for the execution of rebels against Roman rule. As common then as now. My zeal was not strong enough to face that. Rather than suffering physically, I suffered silently and within my soul. I was afraid of them. I was a coward.

My friendship with Lazarus continued. Being close neighbours, we would often visit one another, and sit in the courtyard during the day, or up on the roof in the evening, drinking wine and philosophising. We no longer mentioned armed uprising. That was too dangerous a subject, even among friends. Instead we talked of the Messiah; of when he would come and what he would be like; of the corruption of the Sadducees and the sanctimoniousness of the Pharisees. We agreed on most points and rarely argued.

Lazarus, like me, was fairly well-off. His father, Simon, ran an oil-press in their garden, and business was good. He had two sisters, Martha and Mary, who, although they never joined in our discussions, would often sit with us and listen as they sewed or prepared the evening meal. Martha was the older, a plain girl with a sweet and gentle disposition. Mary, on the other hand, was extremely attractive, but of a pouting, sulky nature. I don't believe I ever saw her smile in those days.

My uncle, as all men must, passed away, leaving me in

charge of the wine business with my two younger cousins. We continued a steadily flourishing trade, even numbering Romans among our regular patrons. Our wine was sweet, although my heart was bitter.

At the age of twenty-eight I became engaged to Martha. The match was to be solemnised the following year. Although I did not love her, I was not averse to the marriage. Tradition had to be conformed with. Like my father and grandfather before me, I would produce children, and when I was gone they would have their own, passing on the business of selling wine to the people. They in their turn to be crushed under the grinding heel of Rome.

Then one day news came to the village that made my heart quicken. A traveller passing through on his way to Jerusalem sat with the idlers under the shade of the tamarisks and told of what he had seen and heard in Bethabara. A man of wild appearance had appeared there on the banks of the River Jordan and was calling for the people to repent – for "the Kingdom of Heaven was at hand". He took those who accepted his message down into the river and immersed them in the water, claiming to be washing their souls as well as their bodies if they were truly repentant of their sins. There were claims that he was the fabled Elijah, come again to deliver the people from the evil of foreign domination and announce the Day of Vengeance. Some even proclaimed that he was the Messiah. His name was John.

For I say unto you, Among those that are born of women there is not a greater prophet than John the Baptist: but he that is least in the kingdom of God is greater than he.

Luke 7:28

C ould he be the one? Had the Deliverer come at last? I was overcome with an ardent desire to see him, but I had learned to be careful of revealing my true hopes and feelings. There were spies and informers everywhere, who would cleverly try to trap the careless into betraying themselves in conversation.

Using the excuse that I was going on a trip to discuss a possible deal with a customer in a distant village, I set out for Bethabara with high hopes.

It appeared that I was not the only one who had heard the news, for on the way I met with others making the pilgrimage to see and hear "the Baptiser", as they called him. Families, couples and loners like myself. I fell into company with one of the latter, a rough farmer who had come to see if what he had heard was true, grumbling that it was about time the prophets came out of hiding. He had heard that this John didn't beat about the bush. He condemned the rich, declaimed against King Herod and called his wife an adulterous whore. I replied guardedly, claiming mere curiosity as the motive for my journey.

We met other pilgrims returned from Bethabara, both elated and disillusioned. My ears were open to the words of the hopeful. Some had been baptised and claimed that their sins had been washed away. They felt reborn and prepared for the coming kingdom. They said that he preached against property. All was to be shared. Poverty would cease to exist. They described John as angry and fierce, but totally sincere. He was an inspiration.

I could not, however, ignore the views of the dissatisfied, who described him as a lunatic. They said he was possessed by a demon. Some asked what good were words and water when it was action that was needed? And there were others who said that he was signing his own death warrant with the things he preached. It would not be long before the authorities stepped in to put a stop to him.

And when we finally arrived at the river, I, too, was strangely disappointed. It was like a sideshow. Sellers of sweets and souvenirs moved among the noisy crowds, hawking their wares. Parties of rich society folk, conspicuous in their ostentatious finery and simpering affectation were grouped together among the poor. It was obviously a great novelty for them to be condemned in public. It seemed the height of fashion for them to go down to the river to repent and be baptised, but I saw no signs of true contrition on their faces as they emerged from their ducking in the water. The poor, on the other hand, showed great sincerity, singing psalms and raising their arms in joy as they waded to the shore.

John himself was a sight to behold. Half-naked in a goatskin loincloth, his skin almost black from the sun, with matted locks and grizzled beard, he stood up to his thighs in the muddy swirling water, crying out in a cracked, strident voice for sinners to repent and come to him to be shriven. His glaring eyes and knotted brow held no invitation for me, but I eased my way through the crowd to be nearer the river-bank, the better to hear him. After my long journey, surely I might gain something from his wild talk that would profit my soul.

As I drew nearer, I saw that he was in dispute with a group of Pharisees standing on the bank, some of them obviously priests from their dress. John was ranting at them, his bony arms pointing accusingly. He called them vipers, and declared that the axe had been laid to the root of the tree. All that did not yield good fruit would be hewn down and cast into the fire. The Pharisees were outraged and demanded to know who he thought he was. His answer, after a short pause, relieved more than disappointed me. He said he was not the Messiah.

One Pharisee than demanded to know if he was Elijah. John said he was not. Was he a prophet? He was not. Looking at his friends in triumph and preening himself on his successful interrogation, the Pharisee turned again to

John with a slightly gentler air, as though talking to an idiot, and asked who he claimed to be, for they were to deliver a report on him.

In a ringing bellow, John replied that he was the voice of one crying in the wilderness "Make straight the way of the Lord", as prophesied by Isaiah.

There was a brief silence before one of the other priests, with an arrogant, upturned nose, asked him imperiously what gave him the right to baptise if he was neither the Christ nor Elijah, nor even a prophet? Reaching down, John took a palmful of water and studied it silently. Then looking up he declared that he baptised with water, but someone stronger than he was coming, whose very sandals he was not worthy to untie. And that man would baptise not with water, but with fire.

At that moment, as though conjured, a burning gust of wind blew down, raising the dust in stinging swirls along the riverside, and causing many to cover their eyes in protection. At the same instant, a half-naked man stepped into the water and waded out towards John. The sky grew yellow, as though a storm were coming. The Pharisees turned to go, pulling their headscarves over mouths and nostrils. One shouted threateningly across the water that they had heard enough, and he would certainly be hearing more from them.

John appeared not to hear them, for he had drawn the man further out into the middle of the river, where they stood up to their waists, the man's elbows firmly gripped in John's claw-like hands. They stared fixedly into one another's eyes. John's lips were moving and the man's moved in reply, but they were too far away for me to catch their words. I could not help but compare their appearances. John was emaciated, big-boned and prematurely wrinkled by the sun. The stranger, on the other hand, was pale, well-formed and slender, his hair long and tidy, and although obviously not an aristocrat, he had an almost kingly aspect to his bearing. Above all, his face, even seen from afar, shone with an extraordinary mixture of innocence and intelligence that contrasted sharply with the demonic fervour of the Baptist's.

They had ceased their conference and were gazing so intently at each other that the crowd on the bank, who had been muttering oaths against the scorching wind and dust, fell silent and turned their curious attention on them. After the men seemed to stare at one another for an eternity the Baptiser's hands suddenly flew up in a flash and came down on the man's shoulders, plunging him forcefully under the brown turbulent water. He held him down as though drowning him, and as he did so, almost instantaneously, the wind dropped, the sky cleared to a pale blue, and the threatening storm had vanished. As the man came up gasping for breath, a bird broke into song in a tree on the opposite side of the river. The transformation was so sudden that I could not help applauding with many others on the shore as the stranger staggered out of the water towards us. Our eyes met as he passed me. I cannot explain the extraordinary feeling that leapt through me as they did so. It was as though he had pierced deep into my soul with a glance and read my most secret thoughts. It was the Master.

It was the first time I had laid eyes on him. Yet somehow I knew that if that stranger asked me, I would follow him anywhere and do anything he told me to do. He was the one that I had been unconsciously searching for, awaiting and expecting all my life. I knew then that I would not go down into the water with John. It was no longer necessary. I had found Him. The one who would clean and heal us all.

Shaking off the elated daze that had fallen upon me, I struggled through the throng in the direction he had taken. I searched and searched, uncertain of what I should say when I found him. But he was gone. After fruitlessly questioning many people, I was told by a careworn woman with a child at her breast that she had seen the man I described putting on his garments and hurrying away, as thought urgently called elsewhere.

I returned to Bethany, my hopes in John unfulfilled. I kept my pilgrimage a secret, even from Lazarus, whom I went to visit as soon as I had washed off the sweat and dust of travel.

I found his house in turmoil. Mary had disappeared. The family had woken that morning to find her gone without a word. She had taken a few clothes and a little money and left secretly in the night while they slept. Lazarus was grim-faced and Martha was sobbing. Their father, Simon, rocked backwards and forwards, hugging himself and moaning about the shame she had brought upon the family.

Speculating on where she might have gone and why, Lazarus voiced his suspicions. The previous day a troop of Roman soldiers had passed through the village, and he had seen Mary giving one of them wine at the house door, talking and laughing, her hair uncovered. Lazarus had spoken to her sharply and slapped her face, at which Mary had flown into a rage, stamping her feet and crying that women were no more than the slaves of men, condemned to a life of servitude and drudgery, and she had had enough of it. After Lazarus had slapped her once more, she had become stonily silent and retired to her chamber, not to be seen again. Martha wept even more loudly as Lazarus said that he believed she might have followed the Roman troop and joined the traitorous band of whores who straggled after them, offering themselves for money and comfort. Simon silenced him with a curse. Mary's name was not to be mentioned in their house as long as he lived.

And so it was. Misfortune seemed to have fallen on Lazarus and his family. A few weeks later, signs of leprosy were detected in Simon and he was sent away to end his life in a colony, leaving a heavy-hearted Lazarus to take over the running of the olive-press.

News reached the village that John had been arrested. He was charged with treason for speaking out against Herod's adulterous marriage and for calling his wife a whore. The Pharisees had fulfilled their promise. And although I pitied him and resented his betrayal, I felt no great loss, having seen him and sensed that he was not the one who would fulfil our hopes of deliverance.

Instead, not a day went by when I did not think of the man that I had seen John baptise in the Jordan river. I could recall perfectly the way he moved, his body, his face, the look in his eyes, and I pondered them fondly, almost like a lover. But my reveries would always end in depression. I knew neither his name nor where he came from. I tried to fathom why he had made such an impression on me, but I could not. Eventually, whenever his image loomed in my mind, I would expel it forcibly by throwing myself into the business, storming around the wine-press, barking orders at the men, finding fault in all they did, and confusing them with my strangely erratic behaviour.

Time passed, and the day of my wedding drew nearer. I tried to muster some enthusiasm for the event, but I could not. Martha would make a good wife. Although far from pretty, she was gentle and attentive, and perhaps later, after years of marriage with sons of my own, I might achieve a measure of contentment. But there was an aching hunger within me now which I knew could not be satisfied by family life.

And then one night, just as I was sitting down to my supper with my aunt and cousins, Lazarus arrived in a state of high excitement and begged me to come to his house. He refused to answer questions, only bade me come, but I could tell from his laughter and shining eyes that no disaster had occurred. My aunt, rather vexed, said that it could surely wait until I had eaten, but Lazarus was adamant, insisting that I come immediately and almost dragging me to the door. My curiosity was stronger than my hunger, so I went with him. It was a warm night, and he led me upstairs to the flat open roof of his house.

Emerging onto the roof-top, I saw a group of men with their backs to us, reclining on cushions in a semi-circle, lit by the flickering glow of oil-lamps. Martha moved silently among them, filling their cups with wine as they listened intently to the speaker around whom they were grouped. Before him lay a girl leaning on her elbow and gazing rapturously up at him. It was Mary.

Ye have heard that it was said by them of old time, Thou shalt not commit adultery:

But I say unto you, That whosoever looketh on a woman to lust after her hath committed adultery with her already in his heart.

Matthew 5:27-28

I turned to Lazarus questioningly, amazed. He grinned and winked at me in mischievous joy, before beckoning silently to Martha, who came to join us in the doorway, her face glowing with happiness. We took cups from her tray and squatted in the shadows as I questioned them. They answered in whispers, not daring to break the concentration of the group.

It seemed that Mary had arrived that evening with the strangers. They had waited outside while Mary came into the house and prostrated herself before Lazarus, begging his forgiveness. Martha and he had naturally been astonished at her sudden appearance after so long an absence, and

Lazarus's anger melted as he listened to her story.

Mary had, indeed, become a prostitute after running away from home. She had left in a spirit of anger, frustration and revenge. Jealous of the freedom and dominance of male society, she had felt she could challenge and equal it. To an extent she had even bettered it.

Equipped as she was with the dual weapons of youth and beauty, she soon gained precedence over the coven of raddled whores she had latched onto, and became much in demand among the platoon of Roman soldiers that they followed. Her charms had been fought over; a man had even been killed because of her; and Mary had experienced a sense of power over men she never dreamed could exist. Working her way up from soldiers to commanders, she soon found herself in high society. A rich Jewish pimp had taken her on and set her up in her own house in Magdala, a village near Capernaum, with a cadre of regular wealthy customers, Roman and Jew, who kept her in a life of luxury and ease, if not of happiness. She was not popular, however, with the people of the village, particularly the Pharisees, who would spit at her if she ventured into the street, and called profanities as they passed her house, threatening her with retribution for her lewdness and collaboration.

Then one day a group of them had invaded her home and dragged her from her bed where she had been entertaining a rich merchant. Allowing her enough time to throw on a robe, they had dragged her out of the house by her hair and through the streets to the catcalls and jeers of women and children who stood to watch on their doorsteps. Her heart beating wildly with anger and fear, Mary had fought and scratched to no avail, until she was dumped, bruised and defeated, in a dusty square before a group of men sitting in the shade of a wall.

Uncertain of her fate, Mary kept her head bowed, staring at the ground under the shield of her hanging hair. Her angry captors harangued and accused in a babble of voices until they realised that none could be heard, and the din subsided, leaving one spokesman to state their case. He, in strident and indignant tone, declared that she was an adulteress who had been discovered in the very act of fornication. Was it not right that she should be stoned to death in accordance with the laws of Moses?

There was a silence, and Mary waited with expectant dread the first sharp blow of the many rocks that would leave her bloody and lifeless. A sob shook her body as she remembered the house in Bethany, her father, brother and sister, and the real love she had known from them, compared to the merely carnal passion of her clients.

The silence continued. She felt the answer to the question like a bowstring pulled tight before the agreed signal for release, but no signal came. Why did they wait before they condemned her to death? Shifting her eyes furtively up from the sanded cracks of the ground, she peered through the curtain of her unbound hair. A few feet in front of her she saw a man's finger moving in the dust. It seemed to be writing something. What, she could not tell. The strokes of the finger were sure, slow and deliberate, with a laconic quality which seemed at odds with the situation. Then he spoke. The tone was matter-of-fact, but the voice was strange, both commanding and questioning, authoritative yet gentle.

"He that is without sin among you, let him first cast a stone at her."

At this there were murmurs from the men, first of satisfaction that there was to be a stoning, but gradually changing to groans as it dawned on them, and Mary herself, that there was no man there, not even in the whole world, who could meet that requirement.

A muttering and a shuffling was followed by silence. After what seemed an age, Mary parted her hair and looked around her. Her accusers were gone. Before her, in the lengthening shadow of the wall, sat the stranger, scribbling again in the sand, surrounded by his friends. Meeting her inquisitive glance, he asked if anyone condemned her. At first she could not answer. He seemed infinitely remote, sitting there so calmly. And his question went to her heart.

"Is there anyone here who condemns you?"

Herself. She condemned herself. The months of wanton debauchery flashed before her eyes, loveless and calculating, selfish and mercenary. No one but herself. The hypocrites had fled, unable to face this stranger's challenge.

"No," she had breathed eventually.

"Then I do not condemn you either. Go, and sin no more." And with that he rose, his companions with him, and walked slowly away down one of the alleys that led off the square.

Without knowing what she was doing, Mary was on her feet in an instant, running after the men, and throwing herself in the dust at her saviour's feet. She wept and begged for forgiveness, swearing to quit her life of harlotry and sin. Without understanding why, she knew that that moment was the most important in her life. She grovelled on the ground, clutching the man's feet, pleading with him to take her home.

Gentle hands reached down and lifted her up, and the man's eyes looked into hers with a deep and unfathomable compassion. He asked Mary where she came from, and she sobbed out her story. When she had finished he smiled and turned to his friends, asking if they were willing to return a lost lamb to its fold. They, too, smiled and willingly acquiesced, and they set out that day for Bethany, two days' walk away.

On the way Mary never left her hero's side, listening enthralled as he talked to his companions and to people he met on the road. He was a prophet, a teacher, and his message was unlike any she had heard before. By the time they reached Bethany, Mary was a devoted disciple. She poured out his message to Martha and Lazarus, who, sceptical at first, had also strongly warmed to the stranger when they had invited him in with his followers to give grateful thanks for the return of their prodigal sister.

And now, Lazarus said, I must meet him too. He was sure that I would be impressed. Martha smiled reassuringly as we stood up and Lazarus led me forward. As we stepped into the light, the talking stopped and all heads turned in our direction. My glance naturally fell on the one in the middle who had been speaking, and my heart leapt with sudden surprise. It was him! The man I had seen John baptise! The one I could not forget! The Master!

And Simon he surnamed Peter;

And James the son of Zebedee, and John the brother of James; and he surnamed them Boanerges, which is, The sons of thunder:

And Andrew, and Phillip, and Bartholomew, and Matthew, and Thomas, and James the son of Alphæus, and Thaddæus, and Simon the Canaan-ite,

And Judas Iscariot, which also betrayed him...

Mark 3:16-19

You remember that night, Peter. You were one of the visitors, along with John, James, Thomas, Matthew and all the others, my dear brothers! But you would not have noticed the way my knees trembled as Lazarus brought me forward to introduce me. And you did not feel the lightning that flashed through my blood as the Master rose and kissed me in welcome. He held me at arm's length and looked into my eyes, as though reading everything in my life, past, present and future. He sat me down at his left, and I learned all that I had yearned to know since seeing him in Bethabara: his name; where he was from; his mission; where he had travelled and preached and the followers he had gathered in his campaign; those he had chosen who were willing to give up their livelihoods to devote themselves entirely to him and his cause. You, Peter. And our beloved brothers. I listened entranced as he spoke, my gaze never leaving his unforgettable face.

I was inspired. All he said was new to me. He spoke not of the hatred and bitterness which had burned for so long in my heart against our oppressors. He spoke of revolt, yes, but of a different kind. A revolt of love, not of violence, and of a complete transformation which must take place in the individual heart before a change in the world could come about. A voluntary rooting out of the weeds of evil from one's soul before the seeds of the Kingdom of God could be sown and flourish. He spoke with such gentleness, such simplicity, that I became utterly convinced. Hatred bred hatred. Love bred love. It was as simple as that. Hatred must be conquered by love. Evil by goodness. He spoke of the Kingdom of God being established on earth, and all men living in brotherhood and peace. No more wars. No more strife. No more poverty.

Martha, leaning over to pour wine in my goblet, whispered shyly that it appeared that I too, like her, had fallen under his spell. And it was indeed as if he had cast magic with his words. And if she and I and these other men had fallen, how many others would not do likewise, their hearts lit with a new and burning hope for the future?

It grew late, and the Master's men, one by one, moved apart and found themselves a space to sleep, but I stayed on, hypnotised by the words and the presence of the man I had lost and found, until only he, Mary, and I were left.

Eventually I dared to speak. I asked him, begged him, if I could not come along with him on his mission? Nothing now meant more to me. If he rejected me my life would be empty and sterile. He looked at me, the light of the flickering oil-lamp dancing in his eyes, and asked if I was worthy of such a task. I replied that I was not. I was a miserable sinner, but I believed in him, and was prepared to devote my life to him and the spreading of his teaching. He smiled and said that it would be hard. Theirs was a life of poverty and toil, of long journeys and often days without food or rest. Would I be prepared to endure that for his sake, without losing hope? I said I would, and a thousand times more, if he would only accept me and let me go with him.

The smile faded from his lips, and he looked at me deeply and gravely. There was a place for one more disciple, he said, but the others he had chosen himself, and now here was one who had chosen him. And yet he would accept me, for having studied and fathomed me, he believed that I was one who would do him great service in the future. And he leant forward and kissed me on both cheeks, calling me "Brother Judas", informing me that they were to set off early the next morning, and that I was to be one of them. He rose, and after gently extricating his hand from Mary's quick, pleading grasp, found the place where John lay and curled up beside him under a cloak, against the chill of the early morning air.

Hardly able to believe my happiness, I rose to seek Martha and Lazarus, leaving Mary, her head bowed, beside the dying lamp.

I found them talking quietly at the foot of the stairs and

told them that I was to become one of the Master's followers and disciples. They looked at each other, but not in surprise. Lazarus hugged me, laughing, saying that he, too, would have volunteered, but knowing that I was the more worthy, he had informed the Master about me before he had fetched me. Martha smiled wistfully and kissed me on the cheek. She said that she was happy for me, that I was doing the right thing, and that our marriage was far less important than the mission. We could wait and become man and wife in the Kingdom of God, and how much more wonderful that would be!

I bade them goodnight and returned home, waking my bewildered aunt and cousins to say farewell and set about deciding what to take with me. In the end I decided merely to change into sturdier garments and take a small purse stuffed with coins. I could not sleep that night because of my excitement, and was ready when the sun arose for my part in the great challenge of the awakening of the people to the Kingdom.

... blind Bartimæus, the son of Timæus, sat by the highway side begging...

Mark 10:46

The exultant joy I felt as we set off in the light of dawn was beyond anything I had experienced in my life before. On the crest of the hill I looked back and saw the small figures of Lazarus, Martha and Mary still watching and waving from their doorway. Tears came to my eyes. Not tears of sorrow or regret, but tears of pride. My life had been meaningless until then. Now I had something to live for. I was the Master's and he was mine, and I would strive with all my might to serve him well. Turning my eyes from Bethany, I hurried to catch up with the ambling group of men, of whom I was now one, on our way along the road to Capernaum.

I need not tell you of life with the Master, Peter. You were one of us. You were there when he preached to the people in crowds great and small. You saw the expressions on the faces of those who accepted and believed in his message. The radiant dawning of life and hope. I need not talk of our failures or our more than occasional hunger, and nights out in the open fields with only stones for our pillows. All of this we shared.

We all looked at the Master through different eyes, and none of us really knew what to expect of him. I think you, Peter, were a little disappointed that he was not more aggressive, a conqueror Christ you would have gladly championed with a sword. James and John seemed more interested in the imagined power and glory they would inherit when the Master established his Kingdom. And several of the others seemed not to understand him at all. I sometimes wondered why he had chosen them, they seemed so dense and ignorant, though innocent and good-hearted.

Of all my brother disciples, I liked you best, Peter. You were honest enough to admit when you did not understand, without fear of rebuke. And you were the only one interested in learning to read, with the help of Matthew and me, when we had time at rest by the roadside while the Master was at prayer. You were a slow but dogged student, and made enough progress for me to be confident that you will understand all that I confide in you here.

I digress, but I must confess that I was jealous of John. I couldn't understand why the Master should single him out for favour over the rest of us. Why he had the place at his right hand at meal times and was fed with sops by his own hand. Why he was always the Master's partner when we slept out on cold nights and needed another human body for warmth. It seemed contradictory to his teaching. Admittedly, John was the youngest, but in my opinion the attention was not good for him, causing him to be spoiled and smug rather than honoured and blessed. I fought to quell my jealous feelings, but it was difficult.

Jealousy is a wicked sin. So is pride, but it is a more pleasurable sensation, and I swelled with it when the Master made me the keeper of the communal purse. Apart from the occasional rare donation from a rich convert, most of the money in the purse was that which I had brought along with me, but it didn't matter. If anything was needed, it was I who would dole out the coins and note down the expenditure. I was surprised that Matthew, who was more used to working with money, had not been chosen, but I was pleased. It gave me an identity in the group. Any recognition by the Master, however small, was like manna from Heaven to me.

Although I have never been in love, I can only compare my feelings for the Master with that particular condition. My fervour for him increased daily. To serve him, to please him, to promote him, became my sole aim and intention. I wanted to share him with the world, for every living creature to live and learn from him and his message. I would wince with pain when he was rejected or scorned by listeners. To me he was a king – the King – and should have been recognised as such.

He was sent by God, and I wanted everyone to know it. But there was something missing. We needed something sensational to blaze his name abroad. Occasionally we would hear stories of other preachers who were about, casting out demons and performing wondrous deeds. But whenever a dissatisfied listener demanded a sign from the Master to prove that he was a true prophet, he would rebuke them. He claimed that it was a Godless generation that demanded signs and miracles, like children at a circus. The true miracle, he said, would be their own changed hearts and their acceptance of the coming Kingdom of God. Nevertheless, I couldn't help feeling that even just a small miracle wouldn't do our cause any harm.

And so, when the Master eventually sent us out on our own individual preaching tours, and I had finished delivering the word to a small gathering in a village square, around a well, or even in a tavern, I deliberately did not disabuse them when they asked in incredulous voices if it was really true that the Master could make the blind see, the deaf hear and raise the dead to life. I replied in the affirmative. It wasn't my fault if they were too stupid to understand metaphors. And they would go away happy, many of them baptised, passing on the stories by word of mouth, elaborating here and there, until the Master would appear the greatest miracle worker of all time. I didn't care. As long as his name was on as many lips as possible, and the great coming liberation was still being preached, I was content.

My particular tour ended in Jericho, but, being a profitable, busy trading town, I found it difficult to command attention in the bustling market square, and was even ordered to move on by irritable stall-holders when I tried to gather a crowd. Instead, I found myself at the city gates with a captive audience of paupers who sat in the shade begging alms from the merchants who passed in and out with their camel trains and laden donkeys.

Squatting before this motley crew, I related to them the glory of the Kingdom to come, omitting references to the blind, deaf, dumb and ill, since most of them were one or the other – some all. Instead, I lay before them a picture of a world that could be: a life without hunger or poverty, where all men were equal, where no man would be homeless or friendless; a world without kings, tyrants or taxes, the wealth shared by all the people, and where the only law was love. Tears sprang to my eyes at my eloquence, and neither was my audience unmoved. There were murmurs and sobs and muttered amens. Some voiced the opinion that it sounded like a dream, but I assured them that it could all be possible if they would only banish sin from their hearts and accept the leadership of the Master.

"I would like to see this Master of yours," said a voice, and turning I saw that it came from an old blind man seated next to an armless mute. Suppressing the impulse to answer that he might find that rather difficult in his case, I promised them that the Master would in fact be visiting their city before too long, and until he did, they should bear in mind all that I had said. Thanking them for their attention, I rose and set off with the intention of returning to Capernaum.

My preaching mission accomplished, I was eager to get back to the Master as soon as possible, but after a short walk from Jericho I felt tired and, tempted by the cooling shade of an orchard of fig-trees which sheltered a small glittering lake, I entered. After slaking my thirst, I curled up under some bushes and fell asleep.

I woke suddenly some time later, disturbed by a sound. Raising the headscarf from my face, I peered in the direction from where it had come. The lowering sun now gilded the grove with a soft golden light, and I saw the figure of a man approaching the pool, dry twigs snapping under his feet, the sounds of which had woken me. He trailed a staff casually behind him, and as he got closer I recognised him as the blind man I had spoken to at the gates of Jericho. I was surprised at the sureness of his footing. It was almost as though he could see.

I soon discovered that he could, although he did not see me, concealed as I was by the bushes. He sat down by the pool and, opening a grubby handkerchief, took out and slowly counted a handful of coins which he had obviously earned from that day's begging. Satisfied, he re-wrapped them, stood up and began to undress for a dip in the water. I watched the old rascal indignantly. There he sat day after day at the city gates playing on the sympathy of gullible passers-by, and earning a most dishonest daily bread. But he was most certainly convincing with his sightless stare. Even I had been taken in!

As he entered the pool, leaving his clothes and money behind on the bank, I decided to teach him a lesson. He waded out in the water, his back towards me. I crept cautiously out of the bushes, snatched his discarded things and quickly returned to my hiding place.

45

After wallowing for a while and wiping the grime from his body, he turned and made his way back to the bank, but before getting there he stopped and stared in amazement at the vacant spot where his clothes had been. He looked around himself in terror. I almost laughed out loud at the expression on his face. He called out, asking if anyone was there. I kept silent for a few minutes, giving him time to cry out more frantically, and then emerged from the bushes carrying his clothes and money. I saw clearly that he had seen me, although he averted his eyes and assumed the blank stare that I recognised. I asked him what the trouble was, and turning his sightless gaze in my direction he replied that someone had stolen his clothes, and would I please help a poor blind man? I told him that he could forget the pretence. I had observed him and knew that he was not blind. I knew that he recognised me too, and I began to harangue him for his worthless lifestyle, threatening to expose him to the authorities, and demanding an explanation for his abominable impersonation. Eventually, with a sigh of resignation, he said that he would explain all if I would only return his clothes and money. I agreed to his bargain and, after he had dressed, we sat on the bank of the pool and he told me his story.

His name was Bartimæus – "Blind Bartimæus" as he was known. Born to a crippled beggar and an alcoholic prostitute, his life had been hopeless from the outset. There had been no thought of teaching him a trade. The family money had trickled in from begging and whoring: enough for supper, drink, and the seediest of lodgings. His father, recognising the potential sympathy-value of a fresh young innocent, had taught the young Bartimæus the art of rolling his eyeballs back inside his head, so that it appeared to anyone else that he was nothing less than totally blind. This he had perfected so well that he had become the chief breadwinner of the family, and after his mother had drunk herself to death, his father had taken the child from city to city, where they had crouched pathetically on the steps of synagogue and temple, reaping in coin the pity of those who passed in and out. Eventually his father had died, and Bartimæus had come to the conclusion that he was not fit for any other profession. Jericho had seemed to him the ideal city for his base, Jerusalem being too big, with too much competition; so there he had settled, appearing every morning at his place at the gate, returning to his hovel on the outskirts every evening. I was the first person ever to catch him out.

He pleaded with me to keep his secret. He was a poor man. He could give me nothing to pledge my silence, only rely on the goodness of my heart. He was in my power. I asked him what he thought about the message I had preached at the city gates, and he replied that the Kingdom of God sounded wonderful, but it would be impossible, men being too desperately selfish in caring for their own well-being to care for that of others. I told him that was because they were the trapped, blind slaves of the materialistic world in which we now lived. They had no idea or hope. They had not been shown the sublime alternative which the Master offered – which Bartimæus must now reveal to others.

That was my condition for not revealing his fraud. He

could continue his sordid, lying life, eking out his pittance at the Jericho gates, but he must at the same time be baptised as a believer in the pool by me, and henceforth preach the message of the Master tirelessly, telling of the marvellous things he had done and would do for the people if they would only repent and strive to establish God's Kingdom on Earth.

He wept and blessed me, kissing my hands and swearing to do as I said. I warned him that I would return to Jericho when he least expected it, and if I found that he had not been doing as I ordered I would announce his deception, and he would probably be stoned to death. Again he swore, and after baptising him I gave him a few coins before setting off again on the road to my beloved Master, my heart filled with a feeling of great accomplishment, the shouted blessings of Bartimæus fading behind me in the distance.

For this people's heart is waxed gross, and their ears are dull of hearing, and their eyes they have closed; lest at any time they should see with their eyes, and hear with their ears, and should understand with their heart, and should be converted, and I should heal them.

Matthew 13:15

Within a few days we were all together again, gathered around the Master. With what joy we laughed and embraced each other as yet another of us returned from our lone preaching missions! How eagerly we listened to each other's stories of our travels, and the hospitality we had or had not been shown. We had been out in the fields scattering the seeds, the Master told us, and soon would come the time when we would go out and gather the glorious harvest.

How proud we all were of our work, although deep down perhaps secretly puzzled. The message had appealed to the poor and downtrodden, who had all to gain from the promised new world order, but had been scorned by the proud and wealthy. Strict Pharisees had talked of

49

blasphemy, and the Sadducees had been totally out of reach. In a country already divided, what would be the outcome of our harvest? And even if it were bountiful, what would be the reaction of our overlords, the Romans? Such questions we dared not ask, but they were always there underneath, and no matter how much we tried to ignore them, we knew that one day they would break out and have to be confronted.

When we later retraced the steps of our individual journeys in the company of the Master, we found, indeed, that our words, like seeds, had taken root, however feebly, and in the villages and small towns that we came to, curious crowds turned up to hear him speak in the synagogues or fields. News of the Master had spread, and those who came were eager to witness this possible Messiah in person, whether they believed in him or not. Our congregations were, on the whole, poor and ignorant, many bringing with them ill and afflicted members of their families in the vain hope that the tales of miraculous cures of which they had heard could be performed on them. Along with them came devout Pharisees, jealous and suspicious of the Master's teaching, eager to trap him in questions on the laws of Moses, in which he might betray himself as the charlatan they presumed him to be. None were successful. The Master spoke in simple parables and stories, which the crowds, whether they understood them or not, at least found entertaining, a far cry from the obscure, humourless cant they were used to hearing from their religious leaders. They would wonder and applaud when the Master, in answer to the cunning questions of the Pharisees, with admirable simplicity made them fall into their traps with his own questions, leaving them squirming and speechless. And then with amazed incredulity, they would listen as he condemned them as outright hypocrites who demanded conduct from others which they themselves had never followed. Shamefaced and furious, they would retaliate by accusing him either of drunkenness, consorting with sinners or collaboration with the Devil. But all their accusations were as weak as water, and they would depart in defeat, allowing the Master to use their behaviour as yet another lesson for us to learn by.

He worked wonders with his words, and many came afterwards to be baptised in his name, but I could not help noticing the disappointed expressions on the faces of those who had brought their sick to be healed. At least one miracle was needed to cement the stone of the Kingdom into its foundation.

And so it was, as we were nearing Jericho, having stirred interest mild and great along the way, that an idea blossomed in my mind. If a miracle was necessary to stir sluggish minds, then the means were with me. Absurdly simple, yet completely foolproof! My brow prickled with sweat as my audacious plan dawned on me. I had to do it! Whatever the results, I must at least try. Using the excuse that I was going ahead to find suitable lodgings, I hurried off, the idea hatching in my brain.

Jericho was soon in sight, and I was in the shade of the lofty gate where the beggars sat crying mournfully to the merchants who came and went. Spotting Bartimæus immediately, I made my way towards him, ignoring the greetings of those who recognised me. Crouching beside him and grasping his arm, I told him I had come. His face grew pale and he stammered out that he had done as I ordered. Every day he had talked of the Master and the promised Kingdom. If I did not believe him I had only to ask the other beggars. They were sick of hearing about it and laughed when he arrived, calling him "Bartimæus the Prophet". He begged me to believe him. I told him to be silent and listen to me, and whispered my plan into his ear.

At first he was incredulous and protested, but I reminded him that he had no choice in the matter, and warned him that if he did not do as I said I would certainly expose him. At this he fell mute and I related my plan again, making him repeat certain details to make sure that there would be no mistake. Satisfied, I told him to remain alert and await our imminent arrival. As a final incentive I thrust a handful of coins from the purse into his hand before rising to hurry back to the Master and my advancing brothers.

Thankfully you were still some distance from the city when I greeted you, breathlessly muttering my apologies. Then, by stumbling strategies, I managed to fall in step beside the Master. Glancing up at the profile of his calm, resolute face, I was almost afraid to speak to him, but summoning up my courage, I did so. I told him that at the gates of Jericho there was a crowd of crippled beggars. One of them, a blind man, would call out to him in the name of David, in recognition of his lineage, and ask to be cured. The Master need only touch his eyes. It would be enough. Would he do it?

He turned and looked at me searchingly without losing his stride. I asked him to trust me, my soul squirming under his all-seeing gaze. Would he do it? Simply touch the blind man's eyes? With a slight raise of his brow his eyes left mine, and wordlessly we continued forward, I confused and unsure.

The city gates appeared, and as we approached, the people around them, entering and leaving, stopped to stare at us. We must have presented a curious sight, a little army of thirteen men striding purposefully towards Jericho without animals or merchandise.

As we entered, people parted to let us pass, and a low murmur of curiosity arose, which was suddenly broken by the cry I had been waiting for.

"Son of David – have mercy on me!" It was Blind Bartimæus. The Master stopped, and we with him. Again the cry came. Some of the crowd tried to silence him with angry words, but the Master asked for him to be brought forward. I hurried to where he was and led him to the Master, who asked what he wanted of him. Bartimæus replied that he wanted to see.

After a pause, during which I hardly dared breathe, the Master inexplicably knelt down and spat in the dust of the road. Then, mixing it into a paste with his fingers, he stood up and wiped the mixture on Bartimæus's eyelids. Then he told him to bathe his eyes in water. Spying an animal trough near by, I led him to it and, dipping his hands into the water, he put them to his eyes. Almost immediately he began to jump about rejoicing, exclaiming at the top of his voice that he could see! He could see!

And indeed, the pupils had returned to his formerly opaque eyeballs as he went around touching things and staring wonderingly into the faces of all around him, viciously into mine. A miracle had been performed.

At first the onlookers were dumbfounded, thunderstruck. But then they gradually found their tongues, and their voices rose in an excited babble. The news spread like wildfire, and more people hurried from within the city, cramming the gate. Other beggars, blind or limbless, shuffled forward, entreating the Master to cure them also, only to be trampled under the feet of the fit and whole, who advanced begging for miracles less physical – wealth, success, beauty, power. Some of them grasped at his clothing, claiming him for their individual needs and fighting off those behind them, until the situation was out of hand.

Turning an exasperated look on me, the Master managed to tear himself away and retreat in haste from the unentered city, protected by his men, who threatened blows to those who followed pleading behind him for many miles. I was elated. My miracle had succeeded. Thanks to me, the Master would be far more famous than he had ever been before!

Then saith the woman of Samaria unto him, How is it that thou, being a Jew, askest drink of me, which am a woman of Samaria? for the Jews have no dealings with the Samaritans.

John 4:9

Not only would the incident help to spread the Master's reputation as a miraculous healer throughout the land, but it also boosted his image in the eyes of you and the brothers. I remember your amazed questions as to how he could have managed to restore the sight of a blind man, and his reply that all things were possible with God. But he firmly stressed that it was not the body of man that was important, but his soul. The true miracle would be the establishment of the Kingdom of God.

Nevertheless, you had been impressed. And although I never mentioned the incident to the Master, nor he to me, secretly inside I nursed a glowing pride for what I had done. Buoyed by the success of Bartimæus's "cure", I kept my eyes peeled for the opportunity of topping it and bringing the Master even greater glory. In Samaria I found the chance I was looking for.

You will remember, Peter, passing through Samaria, we left the Master by a well while we went together to buy food in a nearby village, and we found the woman talking to him when we returned, who called him Christ, and ran to fetch her neighbours to meet him. God knows what they had been talking about. We were perhaps too embarrassed to ask, she being a woman, and a Samaritan to boot. But she was certainly excited, and returned with other villagers who entreated him to stay with them for a while, to which the Master agreed, although several of the brothers were reluctant to break bread with Samaritans.

But stay we did, and late in the evening, after the Master had preached to one of our most attentive and receptive audiences and we had been well fed and royally entertained, I stayed up talking with the Samaritan woman alone, after you had all bedded down for the night.

We sat together chatting quietly as we shared a final flagon of wine under the hanging vine of her terrace. From inside came the faint snores of her husband. They were not officially married. She confessed that she had lived with several men in her time, and this one would probably not be the last. She was a vivacious woman, in love with love; a trifle coarse and gaudy with her cheap shiny bracelets and rings, but honest and direct, and I liked her. She asked me about my own love-life without coyness, but with a flirtatiousness in her eyes that suggested nothing would be amiss if we were to share a few stolen moments of love together.

I answered that my life was now totally devoted to the Master. There had been a girl in the past, and some day, when the Master's mission was fulfilled, I would return to her. She nodded with a smile, saying that the Master was a special man. I was wise to devote my attention to him. He would do great things for us all.

She asked about the girl. Was she cold? Did I find it hard to win her? I replied that we were affianced, but she was very shy, rather than cold. The Samaritan woman laughed and said that she could remedy that and ensure that I had a memorable wedding night. I asked her what she meant.

Looking at me boldly, she told me that she had the reputation of a witch in her village, although she was nothing of the sort. She merely knew how to distil the essence of herbs and flowers that she collected from the nearby hills, and could make them into potions and medicines. She had learnt the art from her grandmother, who had died some years ago. One of her specialities was a colourless liquid, a drop or two of which in the wine of my bride on our wedding day would ensure the loss of all inhibitions and a night of bliss undreamed of by the wildest lecher. It worked even on the most timorous of virgins. I was welcome to a phial as a wedding present. Declining graciously, I asked her what other medicines she made. She rose and took the oil-lamp, beckoning for me to bring the wine pitcher and follow her.

We went into the house and entered a room at the end of a passage. Setting the lamp on a bench, she pointed to some shelves against the wall where rows of bottles, jars and tubes of various coloured liquids gleamed like diluted jewels. Stroking them lovingly, she claimed that they were worth more than their weight in gold. She took down what looked like a jar of plain water, telling me it was the aphrodisiac she had already mentioned. She could not count the number of grateful husbands with beaming faces who had returned to thank her after their wedding nights. Then, taking another container of amber liquid, she said, with an arched eyebrow, that perhaps it might be more to my requirements. It guaranteed an unflagging night-long erection. I laughed and refilled her cup with wine to hide my embarrassment, saying I had no need of such a thing. Pointing to a bright red liquid, I asked what it was for.

She turned again to her potions and began to describe their properties. The ruby? To rid the womb of an unwanted child. It always made her unhappy to administer that one, but if it was the final decision of an unfortunate mother who could not cope with another hungry mouth to feed, she would concur. For future use she might recommend to her the emerald liquid, which would cause her to become forever unfruitful. Or rather, for the husband, the sapphire next to it which would render his seed lifeless. And for the childless, the violet, drunk together, greatly increased their chances of conception.

I asked if they were all concerned with sex and procreation, and she snorted disdainfully. There was one to cure addiction to drink; one to prevent baldness; one to induce temporary bliss and ecstasy; one to cure headaches; one to banish obesity; one, an untraceable poison, which killed instantly; one to render a person into a death-like trance; one to restore memory; one to suppress pain...

I stopped her suddenly, and pointed to a bottle of cloudy white liquid she had passed, asking her to repeat what it would do. She said that a draught of it would send the imbiber into a coma lasting for three days, during which there would be no traceable heart-beat, pulse or breath, and even the most skilled of doctors would pronounce the victim dead. But on the third day the effects would wear off and he would awaken as if from a dream, with nothing more than a slight headache.

I gazed closely at the liquid, and in its cloudy whiteness strange, half-formed pictures shaped themselves. An idea was creating itself in my brain, slowly and unsurely. I asked if she could be certain of its efficacy, and she replied that apart from having proved it on several animals, there was a girl living in a nearby village who had also used it. In love with a young man her parents disapproved of, and commanded by them to marry one she hated, she had come to the woman and purchased the potion. On the eve of her wedding, after secret arrangement with her lover, she had drunk the liquid and seemingly died. After a day's mourning by her bereaved family she had been entombed. Her lover had then stolen her body from the grave by cover of darkness and transported her to his own village, where she had recovered and married him. If I didn't believe her she could take me to the village and introduce me to the happy couple. They already had three children, with another on the way!

I replied that it would not be necessary. I believed and trusted her. And then I reminded her that she had promised me a wedding present. She laughed and asked which it was to be? For the pleasure of the bride or the bridegroom? The bridegroom, I answered.

As she reached smugly for the colourless liquid I stopped her and demanded the cloudy white. She looked at me in surprise. I asked her not to question, but to give me the one that I wanted, as she had promised. With an indifferent shrug, she poured out a measure into a small phial and handed it to me, warning me to be careful. Promising her I would, I offered her money, but she waved it away with a yawn.

We returned to the terrace, but shortly she bade me goodnight and went inside to join her snoring husband, leaving me to form a shape out of the strange turmoil in my mind.

And then the idea was there and recognised, so shocking and daring that it made me gasp. I blessed God, for only He could have given me such inspiration. So far, the Master was known only in Galilee and Samaria, but here now was a plan which, if accomplished, would rock Judea and spread his name through the streets of Jerusalem and the portals of the very Temple itself! Trembling with excitement, I put together the pieces of the scheme. It had to be foolproof.

I rose, gazing at the stars. It was after midnight. If I set out immediately I could be there within a few hours. I would be able to relate my plan and have it either accepted or rejected, and be back by mid-afternoon. There was no time for explanations or consultations. I felt that I must act at that moment while the inspiration still burned in my brain. Concealing the little bottle of precious liquid inside my shirt and hugging it to me, I strode off without hesitation on the moonlit path to Bethany.

Now a certain man was sick, named Lazarus, of
Bethany, the town of Mary and her sister Martha.

(It was that Mary which anointed the Lord with
ointment, and wiped his feet with her hair, whose
brother Lazarus was sick.)

Therefore his sisters sent unto him, saying, Lord,
behold, he whom thou lovest is sick.

John 11:1-3

I arrived in Bethany before the dawn clouds had lost their pink, and felt no guilt about not going to visit my aunt and cousins. This was not a social call. I was on a mission.

Some workers were already turning the olive-press in the yard of Lazarus's house as I entered, and several offered me a sleepy "good morning" as though I had never been away. I climbed the steps to the roof where I had first met my beloved Master, and found Lazarus, Martha and Mary at breakfast. They looked at me in astonishment before rising and embracing me with cries of welcome. Then they bade me sit down and share their breakfast of cheese, olives and honey, which I did with a will, for I was fiercely hungry after my long journey. Enquiring as I ate, I learned that business was good, my cousins' wine was selling well, that life in the village continued as normal. There had been a wedding or two, a few deaths, and several babies had been born. But what about me? What adventures had I been through since I left their humble lives on the great quest for human souls? They thirsted for knowledge of the Master's progress.

I told them all I could remember of our travels, of things the Master had said and done, and they listened eagerly, particularly Mary, whom I hardly recognised. She was as pretty as ever, but all her sullenness had vanished, and her face shone with the innocence of a child as she sat alert, hanging on my every word.

Cautiously, I related the episode of Blind Bartimæus, the "cure" the Master had brought about, and the subsequent reaction of the crowd. Lowering my eyes, I asked them if they censured me for fabricating such a deceit, but on the contrary, they were vociferous in praise of my cleverness. Lazarus laughed heartily, saying that it was a splendid joke, and Martha, leaning forward and patting my hand reassuringly, said that I had merely taken advantage of the situation to increase the fame of the Master. Mary, after remaining silent for a moment, asked quietly if I had thought it really necessary to add this element of charisma? I replied vehemently that I had, for through it, by a single act – false though it may have been – I had enabled the message of the Kingdom to be spread faster than we could have achieved in weeks, even months of preaching and debate. I wanted the Master to become peerless, as quickly as possible, and I would seize every opportunity for making him so. Martha applauded my words, Lazarus clapped me on the back, and Mary glanced at me with a look of guarded admiration. I knew that then was the moment to lay the plan before them.

Warily, I asked them with more confidence if they would have done the same thing if they had been in my situation. Without much consideration, all agreed that if such a unique chance had come their way, they probably would. I then asked them that if a similar opportunity of an unchallengeable, and yet untrue miracle arose, one which would increase the fame of the Master tenfold, would they reject or accept it? Unanimously, they said that they would take the chance.

And so, my hands trembling, I reached inside my shirt and brought out the little container of cloudy white liquid. Holding it out in front of me, I said that their words were brave, but were they prepared to put them into action in service of the Master? They all looked puzzled and asked me to explain.

I handed them the phial and they passed it between them, examining it as I told them about the contents and the effect it produced on whoever drank from it. A sleep, unrecognisable from death, which lasted for three days, after which time the drug's spell wore off and the sleeper was restored to life, healthy and whole. I told of the woman who had made it, and the proofs she had offered me. Still puzzled, Lazarus asked what it had to do with them. After looking behind me to see there were no eavesdroppers, I related my plan as simply and straightforwardly as I could.

Suppose Lazarus were suddenly to fall ill? Suppose he were just as suddenly to die? Martha and Mary, weeping and in distress, would inform the rest of the village, and would come to pay their last respects; doctors and rabbis would confirm his death; after the anointing of the body, it would be entombed. The ritual mourning would continue, and well-wishers would come from far and near to offer their condolences. The house would be a house of sorrow. But then suppose that the Master should arrive a couple of days later? And suppose, on hearing of the death of Lazarus, he should go out to the tomb, order the stone to be rolled aside, and call for Lazarus to come out and return to life? And suppose that Lazarus were to do as he was ordered? Could they imagine the confusion, the amazement, the absolute stupefaction that such an event would cause? I asked them quietly if they understood what I was talking about, as I rocked the phial slowly in my hand, gazing at the revolving milky liquid.

There was a stunned silence, and I knew that they had understood. Then they all began to speak at once, Lazarus asking when they should do this, Martha enquiring if I was positive as to the effects, and what would happen if anything went wrong, and Mary asking if the Master had been informed of the plan.

I answered Mary's question first. I replied that if one was going to give a gift, or perform a service for someone, one did not generally inform the recipient beforehand. It would come as a surprise to them. It was an unselfish act of love, for the glorification of the receiver and not of the giver. I reminded her of the Master's words on charity, of not letting the right hand know what the left is doing. My explanation seemed to satisfy her, for she remained silent.

To Martha I replied that I was not absolutely positive as to the effects of the drug, but I was almost certain, and I had an instinctive trust in the woman who had made it, even though she was a Samaritan. She, too, admired the Master, and wished no harm to his followers. As to anything going wrong, anything was possible, but I would be back with the Master in the Samarian village that evening, and having informed him of the plan, we would be there in time at the end of the three days. We must trust in God.

And to Lazarus I said that we must begin this work almost immediately. As soon as I had left he must feign illness, and Martha and Mary should broadcast the news in Bethany, so that all would know he was unwell. Then, that very night, he should take the potion, so that he would be "dead" by the early hours of the next morning.

In a subdued voice I admitted that I had presented them with a sudden, staggering choice in their lives, and I wondered if they were prepared to make it for the Master, or rather – why not speak plainly? – the Messiah we had chosen to lead us into the long-promised Kingdom of God. Were they brave enough to face the tremendous attention that the miracle would bring about?

They looked at each other in silence for a few moments. Then Lazarus said in a determined voice that he was prepared to go through with it if the others were. Martha and Mary said that they would, but they were worried about Lazarus, for the burden of the task lay upon his shoulders. He replied that, on the contrary, the hardest role was theirs. He would be merely having a nice long sleep, while before them lay days of exhausting weeping and wailing and tearing of hair.

Suddenly we were all laughing and embracing each other, feeling a close bond of togetherness in our conspiracy. We discussed the plan in detail. Lazarus's illness would be unspecific. A fever, a pain inside. Martha would discover his body the following morning. The empty phial must be disposed of. Mary would scream, distraught, from the roof-top, which would bring the neighbours running. The empty cave at the end of the garden would be the tomb, for which purpose it had already been prepared. Only Martha and Mary should anoint the body for interment. The winding sheets should be tied as loosely as possible. These and other things we discussed long into the morning, and I coached them in how they should behave when I arrived on the third day with the Master and his men.

Noon came quickly, and I rose, saying that I must get back to the Master. Refusing invitations to stay to lunch, but accepting bread, dates and a skin of wine for the journey, I kissed them all farewell and, wishing them courage in their task, I set off back to Samaria, turning again on the brink of the hill to see their tiny figures waving from the roof-top.

When I arrived at the Samaritan woman's house in the late afternoon, I discovered to my horror that the Master had gone! When I asked where, the woman merely shrugged. After they had woken and breakfasted in the morning, they had looked around for me, and finding me absent had decided to go on without me. I was welcome to stay for supper, she said, and for the night if I wished.

I said it was impossible. I had to find my friends, and I begged her to rack her brains for any mention of a destination. She thought for a moment, and then ventured that there had been some talk of Cana. I thanked her profusely and turned and set off at once, ignoring her calls for me to wait until the morrow before joining them. It would take me several hours to get there, and darkness would shortly be falling. I had no time to stop and explain why time was so precious for me. I had to find the Master as soon as possible. It was a matter of life or death!

And the third day there was a marriage in Cana of Galilee; and the mother of Jesus was there:

And both Jesus was called, and his disciples, to the marriage.

John 2:1-2

It was indeed late by the time I reached Cana. Judging by the moon and stars, it was well after midnight. My legs were tired, for I had made all haste, worried about the events which had begun in Bethany at my instigation.

The village was quiet and dark as I approached it down the hillside, apart from one house which was brightly lit and from which came the sound of music and laughter. I made my way towards it and, looking in through the gateway, saw that a wedding party was in progress in the courtyard. It was lit by many lanterns and flickering candles, and smoking ropes of incense perfumed the air. Servants passed among the chattering guests bearing flagons of wine and trays of sweetmeats, and the floor was strewn with flowers and green leaves. At the far end a group of men were making music with flutes, bells and drums, and a circle of onlookers surrounded some dancers, encouraging them with rhythmic hand-claps.

I entered and wended my way through the merrymakers towards the clapping circle. With the utmost relief I recognised one of them. It was Thomas. Then I saw others, you amongst them, Peter, and I knew that I was back again in the fold. Joining the clapping, I saw with a shock that in the centre, dancing with a woman, was the Master.

She was several years older than him, her hair covered with a black kerchief, and although prettiness had deserted her long ago, a beauty shone from her eyes, focused as they were on those of the Master. They danced circling one another with arms outstretched, fingers clicking and bodies swaying to the drumbeat. The woman's movements were somewhat clumsy, as though she were not used to dancing, but the Master had picked up the rhythm and moved expertly to it, a smile of huge enjoyment on his face as he gazed into the woman's eyes. A feeling of jealousy rushed through me. I was also rather shocked to see a man and woman dancing together, but the circle seemed to see no wrong, laughing and smiling as they clapped.

Eventually the Master and the woman ended their dance and left the floor to great applause, their places taken by James and John, who changed the pace of the music by whooping, whirling wildly and stamping their feet.

After a few minutes I, too, left the circle and went in search of the Master, whom I found sitting on some steps with a cup of wine in his hand, the woman by his side. He greeted my approach mockingly, welcoming me as "the prodigal son". I hastily muttered my apologies, but he merely laughed. He was in a festive mood and offered me his cup which I drank from eagerly, not only because I was thirsty from my long journey, but also because his lips had touched it.

Indicating the woman at his side, he introduced her to me as his mother, Mary. A surge of both relief and reverence rushed through me and, seizing her hand, I kissed it and pressed it to my forehead. She pulled it away gently and modestly, smiling at me kindly and thanking me for my respects, but her face bore lines of past pain and secret sorrow that her smile could not erase.

Remembering the urgency of my mission, I whispered to the Master that I had to speak to him about a very serious matter, but he silenced me, saying that it was not the time for seriousness. We were at a wedding feast. It was a time for gaiety and enjoyment. And bidding his mother rest, he took me by the arm and led me back to the circle, pulled me into it, and we danced together to the clapping and encouragement of the onlookers.

I forced a smile onto my face. Around me all were happy, their minds on a wedding. Mine, on the other hand, was on a funeral. The delight of dancing with the Master was overshadowed by the dread of what I might have caused if I could not find the courage to tell him what I had set in motion. I knew, however, that it was impossible to inform him that night.

As dawn tinged the sky with light, the party guests began to retire. Those who lived in the village made their sleepy ways home to the calls of waking cockerels announcing the new day – which would be ignored, for the wedding party was not yet over. It would begin again in the early evening after all had been refreshed by sleep. Those who had come from afar bedded down wherever they could find space in the courtyard and in the house.

Tired though I was, I could not entertain the thought of sleep. Eagle-eyed, I watched the Master as he found a place under the palm tree in the centre of the courtyard. After fashioning pillows from the fallen leaves, he lay down beside his mother and closed his eyes. Soon the whole courtyard was littered with bodies as though a recent massacre had occurred, belied by the lack of blood and the relaxed snores of the corpses.

When I was sure that most were sound asleep, I crept to the Master's side and gently shook his shoulder. His eyes opened slowly and blearily, and he asked me what I wanted in a sleepy voice. I whispered that his friend Lazarus was seriously ill, perhaps even dying, and wished to see him. Half-closing his eyes again, he asked who Lazarus was. I reminded him of Mary, the adulteress he had saved in Magdala, and how he had returned her to her brother in Bethany, at whose house he and I had first met. He grunted in recognition, adding that Bethany was a long way off. There were still two nights left of the wedding party, but perhaps a visit to Lazarus might be considered when it was over. Then, closing his eyes and telling me not to worry, he drifted off again into sleep.

An image of Lazarus, awakened in his shroud and scratching frantically against the stone of his tomb flashed before me, and I shook the Master more urgently. He opened his eyes quickly this time and asked me angrily what I was about. I had no choice but to whisper carefully into his ear the miracle that I had prepared. When I had finished he sat up, suddenly wide awake, exclaiming loudly. Those around us reacted to his shout by turning in their sleep but none of them awoke, and I hushed him to be silent.

Beckoning him to follow me, I moved to the gateway of the courtyard and stepped outside, where the rising sun painted the houses of the village in a soft golden light. Within a few moments the Master was with me. He demanded angrily that I repeat my story, and I did so, filling in more details of the plan. I emphasised that we must be in Bethany within two days or Lazarus's life would truly be in danger, locked as he was within the tomb.

The Master's face was grim as he listened to my tale. When I had finished, he began to admonish me in a stern, indignant voice for all that I had done. He said my idea had been foolish and dangerous, and he wondered how I had dared to put it into practice without consulting him. What was I trying to make of him? A circus conjuror? A performer of miraculous tricks which satisfied only ignorant sensation-seekers? They were not the followers he sought. He wanted those who listened to his message of the Kingdom and acted to bring it about without being influenced by cheap wonders. I had done a great wrong.

I apologised and begged his forgiveness, but I implored him to release Lazarus from the tomb. If he did not he would die, and I would have murdered him. I assured him that I had acted with the best of intentions, meaning only to help spread his message to a wider audience. I bowed my head in shame and disgrace, but I felt his hand on my shoulder. Looking up, I saw the anger had left his face, and his eyes were soft with compassion. We would go to Bethany, he said. He loved Lazarus and his family, and was impressed by the misguided sacrifice they had made for his sake. But I must promise never again to do anything without consulting him first, no matter how much I might believe that it would help him or the cause. I swore that I would do as he asked.

Then, averting his eyes from my face, he asked me to promise furthermore that in the future I would carry out any orders which he gave me whether I liked them or not. I must simply trust him and perform his commands. Again I gave my word, and he hugged me tightly with a laugh. Then he led me back into the courtyard, saying we had need of sleep before the journey.

None of the brothers was pleased when they awoke in the late afternoon and the Master informed them that they were to set off for Bethany the following morning. There were still two nights left of the wedding feast, and it was so far away. John complained the most bitterly, but the Master silenced him. He told them Lazarus had fallen asleep and he was going to awaken him. I blushed at his words, they were so near the truth, but the others were confused and there were more grumbles until the Master said that his decision was final. They would spend one more night of merriment and proceed to Bethany early the next day. He instructed me to go on ahead of them to warn Martha and Mary of his arrival, and kissing his hands gratefully I set off at once.

Jesus wept.

John 11:35

Travelling by night is not easy at the best of times, and this time I was not favoured by the light of the moon, which was obscured by heavy cloud, causing me to trip and stumble many times over unseen stones. I tried to stop as few times as possible, but extreme fatigue made it necessary, and it was not until the sun was almost overhead the next day that I reached Bethany.

I found the courtyard of Lazarus's home filled with menfolk some of whom I recognised from the village and others that I did not, muttering prayers, many of them openly weeping. My eldest cousin came forward and, after embracing me, mournfully ushered me into the house.

The main living room was packed with women clothed in black seated on the floor, moaning and wailing, rocking backwards and forwards and crooning laments. Martha and Mary, around whom they were grouped, crouched with their arms around each other, their headscarves pulled over their faces, covered with the grey ashes of mourning.

I made my way towards them and knelt and offered them my deepest condolences, tears streaming from my eyes, so affected was I by the sorrow of all those around me. Martha raised her kerchief when she heard my voice, and her glistening eyes questioned me. I told her the Master was on his way. Her eyes closed in prayerful relief.

"What have we done?" she whispered. "You see how much they loved him."

"Just wait and see," I whispered back. "How much they will love the one who restores him to them!" She shot me a strange, almost pitying glance before lowering her veil and wrapping her sister even more closely in her arms. Slightly shaken, I backed out of the room and made my way up to the roof, where I resolved to stay and keep watch.

I looked at the rock tomb at the end of the garden, covered now by the circular stone behind which Lazarus slept. It presented a scene of deceptive tranquillity, with sparrows chirping in the olive-trees which stretched towards it, and yellow butterflies floating past. Turning away, I gazed up at the distant hill which the Master would descend as he made his way down to the village.

Lazarus had been entombed the previous day and this was the second day of mourning. For everything to work perfectly the Master should arrive on the following day,

76

preferably some time after noon, when Lazarus would have woken from his drugged sleep. And then what wonders would be performed!

Gradually the rhythmic chanting of the men in the courtyard below and the muffled keening of the women, together with the heat of the sun and my own extreme tiredness, made it impossible for me to keep my eyes open, and lying down in a patch of shade, I fell into a deep sleep.

When I awoke several hours later the sky above was a black velvet dome sprinkled with stars. Hunger gnawed in my belly like a rat, but I dared not go down to look for food. The house was in mourning, and fasting was in order. I comforted myself with the thought that the next day the fasting would be changed to feasting with the resurrection of Lazarus. I curled up again to dream, feeling proud that it was I who would have brought it about.

Martha appeared in the morning, bringing me a cup of goat's milk which I drank thirstily. She told me that everything had gone according to plan. She had not realised how painful the experience would be. The real tears, of those she knew and loved, for the faked death of her brother had moved her deeply. She realised that he would in fact die some time in the future, but she felt she had already lived that day.

I congratulated her and Mary on their performances, saying they were worthy of laurels. I assured her that they would not be forgotten when the Master established his Kingdom. She looked at me with red, swollen eyes and asked me what would happen if the Master did not arrive? If something should happen to delay him – an accident perhaps? Lazarus would be trapped in the tomb and die of hunger or suffocation unless we released him ourselves, revealing the deception we had created. Patting her arm reassuringly, I told her to banish such fears from her mind. The Master would arrive in time. We must trust him.

But after she left me her fears remained and became mine. Imagine if what she had said should happen? How could we release him without exposing ourselves? And what explanation could we give once we had? The idea was a nightmare, and I thrust it from my brain. The Master would come. He must come!

Shortly after midday Mary came to me with a cup of wine mixed with bitter herbs. I took it and thanked her without moving my eyes from the distant crest of the hill. She stood in silence for a while beside me, staring in the same direction. Then she informed me that several rich visitors from Jerusalem had arrived to offer their sympathies. They were regular customers for oil and had felt obliged to visit, having known Lazarus personally as a fair trader and friend. I asked her if she, like her sister, were not afraid that the Master might not arrive in time? She replied with nonchalant confidence that he would come. Telling me not to lose faith, she replaced her mourning-veil and went back downstairs.

And sure enough, a short while later a group of tiny figures appeared in the distance and began making their way down the hillside, raising the dust as they came. My heart leapt with joy at the sight, and then just as suddenly froze with fear. Before, I had been anxious that the Master might arrive too late. Now I was afraid that he might have

arrived too early! How horribly embarrassing it would be if Lazarus had not woken and would not return to life when the Master ordered him to!

The sun was going down, casting long shadows and staining the sky a bloody orange. Perhaps the time was right, but I felt that to be absolutely safe the Master's arrival should be delayed for a little while longer.

I ran downstairs and found Martha crouched in the midst of the mourners. I whispered the news of the Master's approach and my own fears as to the timing. She got up instantly and left the house without a word. I followed behind as she ran, her black mourning-garb fluttering in the fading grey of the twilight. After some distance the Master and men were in sight, coming towards us. He stopped as Martha approached, and I saw her fling herself on the ground before him. As I drew nearer I heard her calling him Christ, the Son of God who had been sent to save the world. Then, rising to her feet and bidding us stay until she returned, she hurried off back to Bethany.

I greeted the Master with a kiss, reading no signs of connivance in his calm, steady regard. I was aware of the grumbles and complaints against Martha from several of the disciples, asking why she had left them there to wait when they were hungry, tired and thirsty and her house was so near. I was grateful to hear you admonish them for their whining, Peter.

We sat on the ground and waited for Martha's return. I suddenly noticed that the Master was accompanied by his mother. She had taken out a comb and, seated beside him, was lovingly tidying his hair. Her face was bathed in tenderness, but still the secret pain was discernible. Suddenly, she glanced at me with an unfathomable expression which made me look away. Had the Master confided in her about the miracle he was about to perform at my instigation?

Then, in the darkness which had fallen, we saw the distant flames of torches dancing towards us from Bethany. As they came closer the Master rose, and we all rose with him. Soon they had reached us, and the one who led them, Mary, fell weeping at the Master's feet.

I need not remind you of the events that followed, Peter, but I feel I must record them as they flash before my eyes. How Martha and Mary wept and complained that Lazarus would not have died if the Master had been there. The shock I felt to see the Master himself in tears. The murmuring curiosity of the crowd as they followed us back to the house and through the garden of olive-trees to the rock tomb. Martha's protestations when the Master ordered the stone to be rolled away, saying that the body would have begun to decay. The removal of the stone by you and Andrew, and the blackness of the gaping hole as the light from the flaming torches flickered on the cliff walls around it. The command of the Master for Lazarus to come forth, and the hush that fell upon us all. And then the sudden screaming and panic that ran through the crowd as Lazarus slowly emerged from the tomb like a ghost, still wrapped in his shroud. Several women fainted, and many people scattered, fleeing in terror. Others fell on their knees, praising God and blessing the Master for this unbelievable miracle. He, after embracing Lazarus and removing the cloth from his face, restored him to his sisters, who kissed him frantically, their faces streaming with tears of joy.

We all returned to the house and the courtyard where began a party to outrival the one we had left in Cana, with music and singing and wine and overflowing happiness at the restoration of Lazarus, who, however, was not present himself, having been taken to his bed by Martha and Mary to rest after his ordeal.

During the celebrations I observed the Master deep in conversation with a wealthy-looking stranger. On enquiry I learned that he was from Jerusalem, a member of the Sanhedrin, by the name of Joseph of Arimathea. My heart soared in the hope that we had gained such an influential follower.

News spread quickly through the village, and soon the courtyard was filled with others who had not been present, wanting to see the man who had raised Lazarus from the dead, and to touch him if possible. The excitement became so great that the Master was in danger of being mobbed, so we escorted him to the roof for his safety, allowing only close friends to join us, while the singing, dancing and rejoicing continued below in the courtyard.

Glancing around at my fellow disciples, I noted the expressions of stunned bewilderment on your faces. None of you understood quite what had happened, but you were aware that the Master had done something extraordinary, completely unexpected, and you regarded him with an undisguised awe. Guarded by a ring of wary brothers, he

81

continued to converse with Joseph, breaking off occasionally to acknowledge the congratulations of permitted admirers. How proud I felt that it was I who had brought the miracle about, and this wonderful celebration of the Master's power. I was sure that he must be pleased with me for what I had done, even though he had ordered me never to act behind his back again.

Martha appeared at my side and asked me to follow her to Lazarus's room, and I slipped away with her. Lazarus was sitting up in bed, being fed soup from a bowl by Mary. His room seemed strangely isolated from the chatter and laughter that filtered in from outside. I rushed forward and embraced him, feeling his body strangely light and bony in my grasp. I held him from me and looked into his eyes. He was smiling, but his pupils were dilated, and his cheekbones stood out in a way I had never noticed before. He began to laugh happily and triumphantly, and we joined him until his laughter died out in a long, rasping cough.

Our plan had worked, he gasped. We would gain uncountable converts to the Master's cause. He felt proud for what he had done. But the experience had been terrible. He had woken in the tomb, he knew not how long before the arrival of the Master. It had been pitch black and silent and he had felt very cold. At first he hadn't known where he was, and then gradually it had all come back to him. He had tried to relax and sleep, but it had been impossible, and soon he found it difficult to breathe, as the air in the small tomb was slowly used up. He became obsessed with a terror that the Master would not come, and fought against it with prayers and incantations. Eventually, just when he felt he could stand the cold and silence and darkness no more, the stone had slowly grated aside and light and air were his again. It had been a true miracle for him. And when he had heard the Master's voice calling, he had risen and gone to him with a relief that was beyond description. How wonderful it was to live! How tragic it was that none of us were aware of the miraculous wonder of being alive!

He began to weep with little sobs, his face puckered like a baby. Martha, Mary, and I too were moved to tears and, hugging and kissing him, told him how much we loved him and admired his courage. His sobbing turned to laughter, but it was strangely high and hysterical, and was soon interrupted by a spasm of hacking coughs. Martha and Mary exchanged glances of concern, and Martha, caressing his brow, bade him lay down and rest. He put his head back on the pillow and closed his eyes, breathing with deep sighs.

Martha escorted me to the door, and outside she looked at me with troubled eyes. Lazarus was ill, she said in a trembling voice. I admitted that he did not appear to be well, but taking into account his habitation for the last three days it was hardly surprising. I said that I thought it was probably just a cold. They should keep him warm in bed, feed him with hot soup and drinks, not allow him to become overexcited by visitors, and he should be well again within a few days. I kissed her on the forehead and returned to the roof.

I found it carpeted with sleeping figures. I was not surprised when I remembered how far they had travelled that day and the excitement of the unexpected event that had resulted from their arrival. I, too, suddenly felt unbearably weary and, finding myself a space, lay down and sank into oblivion.

We were awakened early the next morning with the news that a band of Temple police were on their way from Jerusalem with orders to arrest the Master and bring him in for questioning. The news was brought by a breathless servant of Joseph of Arimathea. Returning to Jerusalem the night before, he had discovered that the raising of Lazarus had already reached the ears of the Sanhedrin, who were outraged by its implications, fearing the excitement might cause the people to act foolishly and invoke the wrath of the Roman overlords. They were determined to put an end to the Master and his teaching, of which they had heard from various spies throughout the provinces. Joseph had sent us warning because, after having met the Master and witnessed his miracle, he had become convinced that he was the Expected One.

Having few possessions to gather together we were able to set off almost immediately. The Master kissed his mother and bade her stay, asking Martha and Mary to look after her until his return, which they tearfully promised to do.

Lazarus was still in bed and looked very weak, but his coughing had ceased. Embracing him, I whispered my heartfelt thanks for all he had done. He smiled at me strangely. After his return from death, he told me, he now knew the true value of life, and he intended to live it to the full. I had no time to question his meaning, for the Master

84

called, and with little more ado we were on our way to the hills of Samaria and safety.

Several weeks passed, and after a sojourn in Ephraim we crossed the waters of the Jordan to Perea where the Master preached some of his most inspired and inspiring sermons. And then it was that he announced that we would spend the approaching Passover in Jerusalem.

Jerusalem! The great challenge! The trial and testing place of prophets from long past! The culmination of the mission!

Apart from the great excitement the news caused among us, there was some questioning and doubt. Was the Master ready for the ultimate exposure in the city of cities? Were we capable of spreading the word successfully in such a crowded, cosmopolitan place, especially during the Holy Feast? Would it be the final glorification and acceptance of him as the Master whom all would follow? Or could it end in abject defeat and the liquidation of all we had fought for? We talked long into the night, each airing a different opinion, which was disputed and pondered upon.

None of us knew quite what to expect, but it was with hearts filled with expectation that we took the road back to Bethany, where we were to spend the eve of the Passover and plan the entrance of the Master into Jerusalem.

Now, Peter, if you have borne with me so far, you will have learned the answers to some questions which may have puzzled you, and read much that you know already. Forgive my rambling. I have tried to contain myself, but the memories come flooding back and seem to move my hand across the page despite myself. You may condemn me for the things that I did, but I hope you will understand that I did them only for the glorification of the Master.

However, what I am about to relate to you now – the orders I was given, and the actions I took to counteract the disastrous results that would have occurred if I had carried them out – I'm sure you will understand and forgive. If I had done as he ordered, you would not now be back in Jerusalem proclaiming the resurrection of the Master and reviving souls with his message of love! All hopes, all expectations, all the glory of the harvest would have perished with him on the cross. Please read on. Understand my motives. And forgive me.

Then entered Satan into Judas surnamed Iscariot, being of the number of the twelve.

Luke 22:3

There we were, back in Bethany after perhaps three months, having been greeted enthusiastically by the villagers who came out to meet us. We warned them to keep the Master's presence a secret and they promised to do so. Martha and Mary rejoiced to see us again, and the Master and his mother embraced lovingly.

A message was sent to Lazarus in Jerusalem. I was shocked to learn that he had married and moved there in our absence, but his sisters assured me that she was a good woman, and although she had never met him, was already a devoted disciple of the Master's teaching.

Lazarus had become a minor celebrity after his

resurrection and many people had come down to Bethany to see him. She, the widow of a rich spice merchant, had proposed marriage shortly after their first meeting, and he had accepted without hesitation.

When he arrived without his wife that evening to greet the Master, I jokingly admonished him for his hasty nuptials, but he merely laughed and said he had told me that he intended to seize his chances in life, and if a rich widow was one of them, why then, she was to be seized! He appeared healthy and happy, and I could not be angry with him, but I was disturbed by his flippant tone and sudden mercenary attitude.

We ate and drank well that night, seated on the terrace roof under the stars. A shared elation passed between us, as if our goal was in sight and the morrow would be our making. Talk flowed along with the wine, and plans were laid out. The Master, strangely remote, as though his mind were on other things, gave his orders. I remember your snort of contempt, Peter, when he instructed Philip to go early in the morning and fetch a she-ass and her colt to be his transport, saying that it would be more fitting for him to be astride a fiery stallion for his entrance into the city. We all agreed with you, but the Master silenced us with a quotation from Zechariah: "Rejoice greatly, O daughter of Zion; shout, O daughter of Jerusalem: behold, thy King cometh unto thee: he is just, and having salvation; lowly, and riding upon an ass, and upon a colt the foal of an ass." He reminded us that the horse was a symbol of war, and he had come to bring peace. The scriptures must be fulfilled, he said – a phrase he had come to use more and more frequently.

I managed to change the disgruntled mutterings to laughter by asking him upon which he intended to ride, the ass or the foal? Or perhaps, if the scriptures were to be filled, on both at the same time? The Master, too, smiled at my joke and said that we would see. Then, as he began to instruct us on our behaviour, Mary came to my side and whispered that a visitor had arrived that I should see.

Rising reluctantly, I followed her downstairs, chastising her for allowing an intrusion that we had specifically forbidden. Apologising, she claimed that she presumed it to be important. It was the Master the stranger had asked to see, but she had thought it more appropriate that I should deal with him.

The man waiting on the doorstep outside turned round at the sound of our footsteps. He was no stranger to me. It was Blind Bartimæus from Jericho!

Dismissing Mary, I ushered him into the courtyard and asked him what he wanted. He was dressed in the same rags that I had last seen him in, but the blank stare he had worn in his "blindness" was replaced by a bitter, shifty expression. Looking at me disdainfully, he replied that it was not me that he wished to speak to, but my Master. I told him that he was busy and could not be disturbed, but I would gladly pass on any message he wished to convey. He laughed cynically and asked if I would be so kind as to ask him if he would perform another miracle and make him blind again? Sternly, I asked him what he meant, and he told me his story.

He had lost his livelihood. Before, when he was blind, he had been able to make enough to afford something to eat

89

every day through the charity of sympathetic passers-by. It may not have been an honest living, but he had at least made one. Then I had come along and ruined his life. After his "cure" by the Master he had been brought before the Pharisees and asked to explain the sudden restoration of his sight. They had been outraged by his reply that the Master was the Messiah and had performed a miracle through the will of God. They had thrown him out of the synagogue and threatened to punish him for blasphemy. Not only that, when he had returned to his begging place at the gate, nobody would give him any money. They told him to get a job and stop sponging off others. That was all very well for them to say, but what work was he capable of? He was too old and lazy to learn a trade, and when he looked around at the options open to the unskilled labourer, the choices were not tempting. They were dirty, tiring and degrading. How much more appealing was his old way of life! Simply sitting in the shade against the wall, gossiping with his fellow beggars and relying on the kindness of passing strangers.

The money he had saved, and that I had given him, had soon petered out, and he was reduced to a state of penury he had never before experienced in his life. It was all my fault. I must give him some more money. Otherwise, he said, he would be tempted to expose the miracle as a fake and the Master as a charlatan. I quietly pointed out that if he did such a thing he would also reveal the fact that he had never been blind in the first place, and had spent his whole life cheating and defrauding people. At best, he could expect branding and becoming a social outcast. At worst, death.

His jaw dropped, and he said he hadn't thought of that. I tried to appeal to his better nature by reminding him of the promised Kingdom, and all the wonderful things it would bring, but he silenced me. It was a lovely idea, he said, but when was it going to happen? In the meantime he had an empty belly, and money was the only way to fill it.

Seeing that there was no use arguing with him, I reached for the purse at my belt. I counted out a number of coins, which left the purse substantially lighter, and pressed them into his hand. Peering at them and fingering them greedily, he said that it wasn't enough. He couldn't last for a week on that pittance. Exasperated, I explained that we were going up to Jerusalem for the Passover feast the next day and that was all I could spare. I told him it could be the culmination of our mission, and that the Kingdom might be nearer than he thought. He snorted in derision and said that it had better come soon or he would be forced to have a sudden relapse and become blind again, which wouldn't look very good for the Master. Miracles were meant to last!

I escorted him out onto the street, warning him angrily that he would get no more money so there was no point in seeking us out again, no matter what threats he brought with him. With an obscene gesture of farewell he shuffled off into the darkness, and with disgusted relief I returned to the roof.

I found you had all bedded down for the night to get a good rest in preparation for the morrow. All, that is, but the Master, who was sitting on the low parapet wall, gazing up at the stars. He got up as I emerged from the stair-well and came towards me with a gentle smile on his lips. He asked me what the matter was. I told him of the arrival of Bartimæus and the story he had told me. The Master laughed softly and reminded me that I had acted without consulting him on the matter, so I was only reaping the results of my thoughtlessness.

Then, taking me by the arm, he said that he would like to walk for a while in the garden before retiring to sleep, and he would be pleased if I would accompany him. I was surprised at this sudden honour, for the Master seldom gave any of us, apart from John, the privilege of his individual company. Glowing with pride, I descended the stairs with him, relishing the closeness of his body.

We wandered for a time among the trees, listening to the chirrup of the crickets and watching the erratic dance of the glowing fireflies. The moon was huge, and I glanced occasionally at the Master's thoughtful face, bathed in its silvery light. I was filled with a blissful contentment.

After a while he released my arm and, leaning back against the gnarled branch of an olive-tree, gazed for a while up at the sky. Then he spoke.

In a quiet voice he asked me if I remembered the promise I had given to him to do anything he asked, whether I wished to or not? I said that I did and I would keep my word. There was a short silence. Then he said that when we got to Jerusalem he wanted me to go to the Temple priests and offer to hand him over to them.

At first I could not believe my ears, and asked him to repeat what he had said. Calmly and slowly he did so, and I was stunned. Had he gone mad? I told him I didn't understand. Why should I do such a thing? The Temple priests hated him. He was a threat to their authority. They would arrest him and charge him with some fabricated crime. They might even have him executed! What he was suggesting was dangerous nonsense. After all our work, all his preaching, all the followers he had gained, why should he decide to commit suicide and plunge the movement into dismal failure? I was utterly bewildered.

Putting a hand on my shoulder, he told me to trust him. He had thought the whole thing out and come to the conclusion that it was the only way to ensure our triumph. The Sanhedrin were out to get him, it was true, but they would not dare to have him arrested in the crowded streets of Jerusalem, surrounded as he would be by his followers and admirers, for fear of sparking off a riot that they would find difficult to explain to their Roman overlords. But given the chance to seize him unguarded in some quiet place, they would jump at it. Once in their hands they could try to find any charge they liked to throw against him, but none of them would stick. He was not a criminal. All he preached was love.

I tried to argue with him but he silenced me, saying that he had not finished. I should not worry for his safety. Did I not remember that we were going up to Jerusalem to celebrate the feast of the Passover? And did I not know that Roman jurisdiction had decreed as a concession to the Jewish people that a prisoner of popular choice must be released to them on that day? And who would that prisoner be but himself? The people would demand his reprieve, and they could not be refused, by law. He would be freed by the will of his flock, and by this action more would come to hear of him and join the fold. Could I not see the logic in his plan?

I could. I could almost hear the triumphant hallelujahs and see the Master carried shoulder-high away from his impotent captors by the jubilant crowds. But at the same time I was terribly afraid. What if they tortured or humiliated him? I could not bear the thought. I asked him again to reconsider, but he replied that his mind was made up. I must go the next day to the top officials of the Temple and bargain with them for his ransom, and make sure that I got a good price! He warned me to tell no one of our plan. Total secrecy was in order if we were to succeed.

Another anxious thought came to me, and I voiced it. The others would believe that I was a real traitor. They would shun and hate me. Chuckling softly, he put his arm around my shoulder. Perhaps they would, he said. But it would not be for long. After his release he would inform them that I had been acting on orders and I would be admired and respected for my courage. He had to have his betrayer, and he had chosen me for the cunning initiative I had shown in my previous endeavours. I flushed with embarrassment and could say nothing. Reminding me of my promise of obedience and telling me to be brave and not fail him, he kissed me gently on the cheek and walked slowly back to the house.

I lingered for a while in the garden, my thoughts filled with confusion. It was an audacious plan, but it was not mine, and it had come as a shock to me that the Master, too, could resort to trickery to further his cause. And to put himself in such danger worried me terribly. You can understand my dilemma, Peter. Would you have agreed to carry out such an order?

After long, tortured speculation I returned to the roof and lay down among the sleepers. I tried to sleep myself but found it almost impossible. I kept waking from fitful dozes, remembering with horror what the Master had asked me to do. I dreaded the dawn.

The disciple is not above his master, nor the servant above his lord.

But dawn it did, and after the usual yawnings and stretchings and lazy ablutions, the men were awake with an excitement that heightened with the rising of the sun. None seemed to notice my despondency except the Master, who occasionally cast me an encouraging smile, which did little to boost my confidence. I felt isolated and remote, already an outcast for the deed I was to perform for him.

We ate breakfast; Philip was sent for the donkeys, and Martha and Mary brought out some of the best wine to give us spirit. James and John caused some ill-feeling among us by asking the Master if they could sit on either side of him in judgement of the sinners when the Kingdom was established. We were pleased to hear him shame them into silence by declaring that those who exalted themselves would be lowered and those who humbled themselves would be exalted.

Mary appeared at my side and whispered that a stranger had arrived asking to see the Master. I rose and went with her, angrily berating her for admitting yet another visitor. We were supposed to be there in secrecy, and yet she was allowing open house to all callers. She said she couldn't help it. There was something strange about the man. He looked like a tramp, but his voice was cultured. And she had felt so sorry for him when she had told him that the Master was not there. The expression of sorrow and despair on his face had touched her heart, so she had told him to wait, and decided to call me to interrogate him.

The stranger in the courtyard did indeed resemble a poor beggar. He wore a torn, dirty robe, tied with a rope. His hair and beard were long and unkempt, but his eyes had a gentle expression that reminded me very much of the Master's. I asked him what he wanted.

He said that he had done it. I didn't understand. I asked him what he had done. His voice belied his appearance, being soft and cultured. He said that he had done what the Master had told him to do. He had sold all his possessions, given the money to the poor, and come to follow him. He had been searching for him for so long. Did I not recognise him?

And then suddenly, to my astonishment, I did. But his appearance was so altered from the last time we had met that he seemed an entirely different person.

It was the rich young man who had come to see the Master while he was preaching in Decapolis. He was the son of a wealthy governor, and had approached the Master after one of his sermons, asking him how he could gain eternal life. He had been clad then in costly and beautiful clothes, decorated with gold and jewels, his hair oiled and dressed, his body fragrant with perfume. He had spoken to the Master humbly and reverently, but had addressed him as "Good Master", to which the Master had retorted that nothing was "good" but God. If he wished to gain a place in Heaven he should follow the Commandments strictly. The young man replied that he had obeyed them throughout his life. At this the Master had smiled warmly and announced that if that were so, there was but one thing lacking. He should renounce his wealth, sell all that he had, give the money to the poor and then come and follow him. There was a silence, and the young man had sadly lowered his eyes and slowly walked away.

The Master had told us to observe how difficult it was for a rich man to enter Heaven. It was easier, he said, for a camel to pass through the eye of a needle than for a rich man to get into the Kingdom of God.

And there he stood before me, our rich young man, stripped of all his finery, dressed in beggar's rags, abased and humbled. He had returned home after his conference with the Master, he said, and spent several days in troubled contemplation before coming to his decision. Then, casting all doubts aside, he had put the Master's words into action, generously paying off his servants, freeing his slaves and selling off his property to the usurers who came swarming like flies when they heard of the bargains to be had, until everything was gone. Then he had distributed the money among the astonished poor of his province.

His father, hearing of his deeds, had come to reason with him, but seeing how adamant he was, had given him up in despair, disowning him and cursing him for a fool. But he had not cared. He had even exchanged the last of his rich garments with those of a poor beggar he had met on the road. He felt richer now with nothing, having disposed of all of his wordly cares along with his money. He felt reborn. His only concern was to find the Master and join him, and that he had set out to do. He had searched and enquired along the way for news of the Master and been directed to different locations, only to be told that he had left days or hours before, and so his quest had stretched on endlessly. But the burning hope of finding him had kept him resolute, no matter how hungry and exhausted he had become. And had he found him at last? Or could I tell him where he might be? He looked at me pleadingly.

Without a word I took him by the arm and led him up the stairs towards the roof. I could find nothing to say, so impressed was I by his faith and devotion. I was in awe of him for the incredible sacrifice he had made for the sake of the Master. There was no question of turning him away; his perseverance had to be rewarded. I guided him out into the sunlight and the presence of the Master, who stood with cup in hand, finishing some amusing anecdote, for you all laughed when he stopped speaking and continued to do so until aware of an alien presence, at which you broke off and stared silently and suspiciously at the stranger with me.

As I brought him forward, he broke away from me and ran and knelt before the Master, grasping his hand and kissing it feverishly. The Master stooped and, raising him to a standing position, gently rebuked him. No man should kneel before another, he said. Then he glanced questioningly at me. I said that this was a visitor that I could not find it in my heart to turn away. When he had heard his story he would know why.

And so the young man related the same tale he had told me downstairs to the Master and you, my brothers. We learned his name. It was Darius.

When he had finished there was a pause. Tears were in the Master's eyes, but he was smiling. He opened his arms wide and embraced Darius, kissing him lovingly on both cheeks. Then, turning to the rest of us, he announced that we were witnessing a true miracle. A camel had passed through the eye of a needle! Here was a true believer, ready to sell all to buy the pearl of great price, one who had sacrificed more than any of us to gain eternal life.

Forgive me, Peter. Again I am relating events at which you were present. But owing to the great debt that we all owe Darius, I cannot avoid recording his meeting with the Master and the effect it had upon us all.

Darius staggered, and seemed on the point of collapse. The Master helped him to sit down and asked how long it had been since he had last eaten. Darius replied that he had been given some bread by a passing traveller two days before. The Master told Martha to bring him something immediately, and he put his own cup of wine to Darius's lips, helping him to drink. I could not control a smile of pleasure at the peevish look of jealousy on John's face.

After he had eaten some bread, cheese and fruit, Darius was taken downstairs by the Master and Lazarus, and when they returned with him a short time later he was transformed. His face had been washed, his hair and beard trimmed, oiled and combed, and he was dressed in one of Lazarus's clean white robes. Again I was struck by his resemblance to the Master, in their features, bearing, and the air of peaceful tranquillity that radiated from their eyes. They might even have been taken for brothers.

When we sat down, the Master placed Darius at his right hand, at which John could contain himself no longer, complaining that he had always sat on the Master's right. The Master told him not to be jealous, and reminded him of all that Darius had sacrificed for his sake. He had totally humbled himself, and for that reason he must be loved, honoured and blessed. John folded his arms and sat seething, his mouth a grim line.

Martha and the Master's mother brought bowls of pottage and bread as a final meal before we set off, and we ate in silence, each with his own private thoughts. The Master fed Darius with his own hand, smiling at him lovingly.

Suddenly Mary appeared and slowly approached the Master. Standing behind him, she broke open a small flask of nard that she was carrying and poured it over his head. We were all stunned by her unexpected action. John pushed her roughly away with an oath. The sweet smell of the perfume reached me, and I admonished her angrily for her waste. From its scent it was obviously expensive. We would have done better to have sold it and given the money to the poor. You all murmured in agreement, indignant at her extravagance, but the Master said that she had done a beautiful thing. The poor would always be there for us to help, but he would not. She was merely anointing him in preparation for his burial. And was not the expected Messiah also known as the anointed One? Yes, muttered Thomas, but not by a whore. And you, Peter, complained that she had made the Master smell like one.

I could say nothing. My blood had frozen at his words of anointing and burial, reminding me of the task that lay ahead of me in Jerusalem. Who could predict what would happen once I had turned his willing body over to the wily priests of the Sanhedrin?

At that moment Philip appeared in the stair-well to announce that the donkeys had arrived. The Master asked him to rest and drink after his tiresome mission, but he declined, saying that he had already drunk with the donkeys' owner and was anxious to be on the way to Jerusalem, as time was passing.

And so the Master rose, and all of us with him. After kissing Martha and Mary, he bade them keep his mother safe until his return. She, crying and clinging to him, begged him not to go, for she had had a dream of ill-foreboding, but he removed himself gently from her hold and, kissing her on the forehead, told her not to worry. He promised that he would return soon. Wishing the three women a happy Passover, he descended the steps to the street, and we all followed.

A crowd of villagers were waiting outside, holding palm

branches which they waved when the Master appeared, and cheering and clapping. The Master told us to gather palms along the way and do likewise, and ordered some of the brothers to go ahead to the gates of Jerusalem to announce his arrival. If any of us got separated in the city, which was possible with the multitudes that would be there, we were to meet that evening at the house of Joseph of Arimathea, who had offered us a room for our Passover supper. Then he blessed us and said that we were all to act strictly according to the instructions he had given us. He looked meaningfully at me when he said this, and my heart sank. He was still determined that I should betray him.

I remember you, Peter, complaining about the manginess of the two donkeys and asking if better could not have been found? You said they were unworthy of the Master and would make him an object of ridicule, but he merely smiled and stroked the muzzle of the she-ass, saying that they would suffice. Then, putting his arm around Darius, he announced that he would ride beside him on the colt. He was still exhausted from his long search, and it would unduly tire him to walk the two or more miles to Jerusalem. John let out an involuntary yelp of rage, but suppressed himself after a look from the Master. Darius protested that he was not worthy of such an honour, but the Master said that he was worthy of more, and if he would not accept it he would let him ride the she-ass and he would ride the colt, at which suggestion Darius mounted the young donkey without demur. An enthusiastic villager spread his cloak over the back of its mother, the Master took his seat, and with a wave of his hand we were off.

A small crowd of the folk from Bethany accompanied us, singing and chanting and throwing their cloaks under the hooves of the Master's beast to cushion his step and, no doubt, to brag in later years that they owned a cloak over which the Master had ridden on his triumphant procession to Jerusalem.

The young foal, alarmed by the noise, kept close to its mother, so Darius and the Master rode abreast, and although Darius's feet almost touched the ground and the Master was bounced up and down, they could not be deemed a ridiculous sight due to the calm and resolute expressions upon their faces.

And then, as we rounded the crest of a hill, Jerusalem suddenly came into view. The Master halted his donkey, and we all stopped our chanting and stared in silence at the city. I had seen it often enough in the past, but never ceased to be impressed by the sight. From its strategic position, thick protective walls rose majestically, surrounding towers, roofs and turrets, and the magnificent golden dome of the Temple glittering in the sun. We could see tiny figures streaming in and out through the gates. Their calls, chants and chatter reached our ears like the faint humming of a beehive. Many of our brothers from Galilee, you included, Peter, had never seen Jerusalem before, and your mouths hung open as you gazed in awe at the holy city.

Turning to the Master, we were astonished to see that he was weeping. He gazed ahead, tears rolling unchecked down his cheeks. In a choking voice he cried that they would never accept him. This was Jerusalem, the city which murdered the prophets and stoned the messengers

God sent to her. Its inhabitants were blind, and they and the city would all be destroyed because of their refusal to accept the true word of God.

Many of us rushed to his side to comfort him with reassuring words. He would be recognised. We were looking upon the city where he would be enthroned, and from which he would rule in righteousness and justice. Others may have suffered there in the past, but God would protect him. He was the Chosen One. He need fear no harm..

Wiping his eyes silently with his sleeve, the Master spurred on the donkey with his heels, while I stood and watched for a moment as the little band of dusty followers resumed their chanting and palm-branch waving around the two men on their bony, stumbling donkeys. They seemed, suddenly, heartbreakingly pathetic, and the Master's talk of murdered prophets and stoned messengers sent a shiver of foreboding down my spine.

*Then one of the twelve, called Judas Iscariot, went
unto the chief priests,*

*And said unto them, What will ye give me, and I
will deliver him unto you? And they covenanted
with him for thirty pieces of silver.*

*And from that time he sought opportunity to
betray him.*

Matthew 26:14-16

O ur entry into Jerusalem was not the triumphant
occasion we had imagined it would be. The
gateway was crowded with pilgrims and traders
coming and going, but we managed to create a lane for the
Master and Darius by marching on either side of them,
waving our palm-leaves and shouting hosannas, forcing the
people to step aside.

A small group of followers had gathered to welcome the
Master with cheers, but they were far outnumbered by the
other folk going about their business, who seemed puzzled
and irritated by the temporary obstruction we were
causing. Many stopped to stare at our curious procession.

Others came forward to ask what was going on. I told them that the Messiah had come, the King of Righteousness who was to deliver our country. One man asked which one he was, and, glancing at the Master and Darius riding along side by side, I could understand his confusion. A street trader arched his eyebrow cynically at my reply and exclaimed, "Not another one!" When I asked what he meant, he said that he had already witnessed the arrival of three other Messiahs and their followers that day. He laughed and slapped me on the back, saying, "May the best man win!" and went back to hawking his wares.

As we emerged into the huge square before the Temple I noticed that our arrival seemed to be only another Passover distraction, and the choice was manifold. The square was crowded and noisy, with money-changers, food and drink vendors, sheep, goats, cows, camels and birds to be purchased for sacrifice. Crowds of people surrounded various speakers who stood here and there on upturned barrels: Zealots, Essenes, Pharisees and general rabble-rousers, haranguing their listeners with different messages.

We stopped and the Master and Darius dismounted. With a conspiratorial wink, the Master told me to be about my business, and then, with an arm around Darius, he gestured to the rest of you and strode forth into the thronging crowds of the square.

I was left alone, and looking up at the towering magnificence of the Temple I could understand why the mouths of my brothers had hung open. There is probably not a more impressive building in the world, and I felt tiny and humble as I mounted the steps and made my way through the beautiful cloisters of marble to the upper level and the Temple proper.

Although the outside of the Temple is magnificent, the inside is stomach-turning. The mingled odour of freshly spilled blood and cloying incense, and the droning sacred chants of the Levites, half-drowned by the frantic screams of the sacrificial beasts in the darkling gloom, has always seemed to me like a scene from a nightmare. I had to hold my breath to stop myself from vomiting.

I found an idle Temple priest leaning against a pillar and told him that I wanted to see one of the top officials. He looked down his nose and asked me my business. I said that it was none of his, but I had some information to convey in which they would be very interested, and if he took me to one of them he would probably be rewarded for it. With a disdainful sniff he signalled me to follow him, and I did so, down many a grand corridor that flanked the Temple, before being ushered into a chamber hung with gold and crimson drapes. In it sat a group of High Priests, laughing boisterously together as they counted piles of gold and silver coins which had been exchanged for the sacred shekel of the Temple by visiting pilgrims, to purchase their sacrificial animals. Their laughter ceased and they looked warily up as I was brought in by the suddenly obsequious underling, who gushed that he believed I had news to relate that might be to their advantage.

All eyes were on me, and there was an expectant silence. As I looked at their bloated bodies in their rich robes, the oiled and curled beards which hung from their over-fed faces, and the greedy, haughty looks in their eyes, I felt a sudden surge of anger and wanted to scream out what parasites and hypocrites they were. That their elaborate rituals and rigmarole were simply meaningless trash with which they deluded our people for their own gain. But I could not. I had promised the Master to follow his instructions expressly, whether I understood them or not. So instead I stammered out that I was willing to betray a man in whom I believed they had some interest.

With an air of detached boredom, one of them asked for his name, while another slipped out a ledger, dipped a reed into ink, and wrote as I gave the Master's name. The others listened, and one or two said they had never heard of him. The inscriber smugly mentioned Galilee, and the ignorant ones gave little murmurs of recognition. Then he turned to me and asked what charges could be brought against him.

I had not been prepared for that, and I groped for words. He preached liberation, I said. Revolution against Roman rule. Universal love and brotherhood. The reed scratched across the parchment, and, after a pause, the High Priest looked up and asked if I considered such charges worthy of his arrest? I hesitated. They didn't seem to be enough. I answered that many people had called him the Messiah, and he had not denied it.

The reed flew across the page with a flourish, and the writer looked up with a satisfied smile to ask my name and place of abode. I said that I refused to give either until the reward was in my hands. At this, knowing looks passed between them. I was told that so many had been in offering to betray trouble-makers in the past, only to disappear without fulfilling their obligations once they had been paid, that a new rule had been introduced. Money would not change hands until the victim was safely in theirs.

I asked how much I could expect, and was told that I would receive thirty pieces of silver. I gasped in surprise. It was a pittance for a man like the Master, and I told them so. They shrugged and said that I could take it or leave it. They weren't made of money. It was their fixed fee for betrayals, and they weren't prepared to increase it for me or anyone else. Saying that I would think about it, I turned and left the room, escorted by the priest who had brought me to them.

I felt dirty as I left the Temple, as though I had been tainted by the presence of the smug hypocrites I had held conference with. I prayed that the Master would change his mind. Surely he would not allow himself to be handed over to them for a mere thirty pieces of silver?

For the first time I dreaded an encounter with the Master. I dawdled reluctantly on my way to the Upper City, where I had learned the house of Joseph of Arimathea was situated. It was late afternoon when I reached it, and as I entered the gates I was astonished that we were to be entertained in such a grand mansion. However, I was met at the front door by a servant who directed me to the stable, above which a room had been made available for our Passover supper.

Mounting the stairs, I found a large room used for storing tools, in the centre of which space had been cleared for a long, low table upon which sat platters and goblets ready for our meal.

Apart from Darius, who was standing at a small, grilled window gazing out over the roof-tops of the city, no one else was there. He turned and greeted me with a smile. I asked him where the others were and he replied that the Master had given them permission to go out and see the sights of the city without him. He told me that I had missed the scene in the Temple square after I had left them. The Master had lost his temper and kicked over the tables of several money-changers and released doves from their cages, and many of the brothers had copied him until they had been chased away by an angry crowd. The Master was on the roof praying, but he had given orders for me to go to him as soon as I arrived. He pointed to a doorway at the back of the room. I went through it and climbed up a ladder, my legs trembling.

The sun was going down as I emerged on the flat roof, painting the sky in glorious shades of red and pink. In the distance the marble columns of the Temple glowed with a rosy light and the gold of its dome shone like fire. The Master knelt in the middle of the roof, his eyes closed. His face was calm and peaceful, and his lips moved silently as though he spoke to some unseen listener. I felt like an intruder, and was about to creep away again when he suddenly opened his eyes and saw me.

He stood up and I went to him. After embracing me briefly in welcome, he looked laughingly into my eyes and asked how much I had got for him. I told him of my encounter with the priests and the amount they had offered me, payable only on delivery. The smile left his face and his eyes flashed angrily. It was an insult, he said. It was the standard price of a slave! My heart rose in hope, and I said that of course he would not agree to be sold for so little. We would abandon his scheme. He looked at me darkly and said that we would certainly not. The money was not important. We would continue the plan, and I would hand him over to them that very night!

I fell to my knees and implored him not to go through with it. I told him of the loathsome feeling I had had in their presence. They were vicious and cruel. I could not bear the thought of being the instrument for delivering him into their hands. But he was adamant, and raising me up firmly he told me to take courage. He would not be long in their clutches. Had I forgotten the Passover amnesty? He would be released by popular demand the following day and could not be arrested again. Could I not imagine how those hypocrites would squirm at the dawning of the Kingdom of God, knowing that their own greed and cunning had helped to bring it about? I pleaded and protested, but he silenced me firmly and reminded me of my promise to do all that he ordered without question. Then he outlined the plan for his arrest.

I was to share the Passover supper that evening with the rest of the brothers so that there would be no questions about my absence. During the meal the Master would give me a signal to leave and return to the Temple officials. He would dip a piece of bread in the sauce bowl and hand it to me. Then I must get up immediately and go. That night he and the men would be sleeping in the Garden of Gethsemane, just outside the city walls. He would remove himself a little distance from the others in the company of

Peter, James and John. And Darius too, he added as an afterthought. I would lead the Temple police to the garden and find him there. In order that there should be no confusion as to whom they should arrest, I should inform them that the Master was the one I would approach and kiss in greeting. Then he would be seized, and what happened thereafter was in the hands of God.

It was simple and straightforward, yet I was terrified of what might happen thereafter. I began to stammer out my doubts and fears, but he silenced me again, telling me to trust in him and the Father. Then he told me to leave him as he wished to be alone to pray. He kissed me on both cheeks, saying that was how I should identify him that night in the garden. Then he knelt down and closed his eyes, and realising that I could do nothing to dissuade him, I left the roof and descended the ladder, feeling the most miserable creature in existence.

The others had still not arrived, and Darius, like the Master, was kneeling quietly in prayer when I entered the room. Seeing me, he got up and came to me, asking what was wrong. My face obviously betrayed my fearful thoughts. He put an arm around my shoulder, and being unable to control myself, I burst into tears. He led me to a low platform and sat me down, murmuring soothing words and patting me gently on the back. Gradually I managed to calm myself, and again he asked me what the problem was. I replied that I could not tell him. I had been forbidden to tell anyone. Darius asked if it concerned the Master, and when I replied that it did, he begged me to tell him, saying that he would keep what I told him a secret, and that a problem shared was half resolved. His voice was so kind and concerned that I could not stop myself. I told Darius the whole story of the Master's plan and the orders I was reluctantly forced to perform.

He sat in silence when I had finished, staring into space, his face troubled. Then he spoke. I must not do it, he said. They would kill him. If I delivered him into their hands it would be the end of the mission. Once they had him they would find a way of getting rid of him, even if the whole of Jerusalem clamoured for his release. He was a thorn in their side that they wished to remove at all costs. It was suicide for the Master to submit to them. I told him I agreed with him, but what could I do? He had ordered it.

Darius rose, saying that he would go and speak with him and persuade him to change his mind, but I clung to his sleeve and begged him not to. I had already put forward all arguments against his scheme, but he was determined, and he would be furious with me for confiding in another against his strict instructions.

Darius sat down again and was silent for a while. Then he said that he could see only one other alternative. Eagerly, I asked him what it was. He replied that I should not hand over the Master, but a substitute. Himself.

Before I could speak, he quickly outlined his plan. I must kiss, not the Master, but Darius, who would then be seized and taken away, leaving the Master free.

I was so stunned that I could not speak for a few seconds. Hope welled up in my heart like the waters of a hot spring. I admitted that it could work. The Master was not known to the priests by sight, only description, and that of Darius was very similar to the Master's. But was he willing to go through what they may inflict upon him? Humiliation, torture, perhaps even death?

Darius said he was. The Master was everything to him. For him he had given up wealth and title, and been disowned by his family. Every blow struck against him would be one the Master had been spared from, and his death instead of the Master's would be the ultimate blessing, leaving him alive and free to continue spreading the message of the Kingdom. And he remembered, he said, the Master's words that no love was greater than to lay down one's life for one's friend.

Suddenly aware of the arrival of you, my brothers, by an approaching chorus of discordant psalms, I quickly told Darius that I would do as he suggested. I would kiss him in the garden and spare the Master. But while under arrest, I warned him, he must remain absolutely silent and not utter a word to betray himself or the Master, no matter how provoked. That way no positive charges could be brought against him. And if he behaved gently and nobly, as he did now, he might win the respect of his captors. His release was not unfeasible either at the granting of the Passover amnesty, if the crowd believed him to be the Master. Darius replied that he would put his trust in God. I embraced him lovingly and gratefully, as you, my brothers, staggered up the steps and into the room, filling it with song.

You will remember that last supper we all shared together, Peter. It remains etched upon my mind. I remember Joseph entering with servants bearing food and wine to apologise sheepishly for not being able to entertain us in his own house. He had other guests to whom he was obliged, and he hoped we understood that in his position to be seen in the Master's company might make things difficult for him. The Master laughed and forgave him, saying that the day was coming when we would all be able to sit down together in God's Kingdom without fear or shame. Joseph kissed his hand and left, wishing us a happy Passover.

I remember the embarrassment we all felt when the Master insisted on washing our feet. We could not understand his meaning, and it was hateful to see him abase himself before us. He told us that it was a lesson in humility. If he, our Master, could do such a thing for us, we should be prepared to do the same thing for each other. Neither did we understand when he called the bread his body and the wine his blood, and, passing it around, bade us eat and drink him.

And none of you understood when the Master announced that one of us was going to betray him. I flushed hotly at his words, not having expected them. I flashed a conspiratorial glance at Darius and he returned it, while the rest of the brothers stared at each other in shock and dismay, murmuring in disbelief. You, Peter, turned to Darius, who was sitting in the honoured place at the Master's right, and asked him to enquire which of us he meant. Darius leaned towards him and asked who his betrayer was to be.

The Master answered that it was the one he was going to give a piece of bread to after he had dipped it in the dish.

Then he tore off a piece from a loaf, dipped it in the sauce and handed it deliberately across the table to me. The room fell silent. I took the crust with a trembling hand and sat there staring at it, not daring to look up.

The Master's voice, sharp and commanding, roused me from my trance, telling me to be quick about my business. I stumbled up blindly from the table, and without a word went quickly out into the night, the damp bread still clutched in my hand.

Then Judas, which had betrayed him, when he saw that he was condemned, repented himself, and brought again the thirty pieces of silver to the chief priests and elders,

Saying, I have sinned in that I have betrayed the innocent blood. And they said, What is that to us? see thou to that.

Matthew 27:3-4

As I made my way down through the dark streets towards the Temple, a fierce indignation burned in my heart. The Master had exposed me in front of all my brothers! He had not mentioned that as part of his plan. I had presumed that all would have been performed covertly, but instead he had talked openly of betrayal and explicitly branded me as the traitor with his overly-dramatic gesture of handing me the piece of bread.

I put it into my mouth and clenched it between my teeth as I walked quickly on, trying to suppress my feelings of outrage. A hellish business lay before me, and I thanked God that he had sent Darius as a willing scapegoat to save the unsuspecting Master's life. I shuddered to imagine what my feelings would have been had he not volunteered himself, and had I really been on my way to betray the Master.

It was late when I arrived at the Temple, but there were still several sacrifices going on, and I found the priest who had helped me before, yawning and leaning lazily against the same pillar. I told him I had come to my decision and was ready to betray the Master.

He turned without a word, and I followed him down the same corridors, now illuminated by flaming torches, to the room where I had been interviewed before. I recognised some of the High Priests I had spoken to, but others were new to me. This time they were not as condescending when I stated my mission. News of the Master's behaviour among the money-changers in the market-place had reached their ears, and they were more eager than ever to put a stop to him. The Chief High Priest, Caiaphas, had also heard of it, and had been particularly incensed. He wished to interview the Master personally, and it was to his house he was to be conveyed after his arrest.

I told them where the Master was to be found and my method of identifying him. I was led to a courtyard where Temple police were lolling and drinking. There were reluctant groans when they were told they were to make an arrest. It was late, they complained. They asked if it couldn't wait until the next day, but they were silenced by the angry bark of a High Priest, and stood sullenly to attention. They were an ugly bunch of thugs, and some of them were obviously drunk. The High Priest shouted more orders and, after fetching their swords and staves and taking burning torches and lanterns from the walls, they fell into rank. Then, after the priest had explained their mission, they were told to follow me. The criminal they were to arrest was the man that I would kiss.

I felt horribly conspicuous as I led my little army of ruffians, many of whose muttered curses and complaints I could hear above the tramp of their feet. Mercifully, the streets were dark and almost deserted, and it was not far from the Temple to the city gates. Soon we were outside and marching down the hill to the Garden of Gethsemane. My heart pounding, I prayed that everything would go to plan.

The light from the torches illuminated the trees as we walked through the garden, and the gnarled branches cast sinister moving shadows on the ground. Eventually we came to a clearing and there, on a small hillock, stood the Master. You and Darius stood on either side of him, watching our approach. James and John were there too, their faces wild with terror, as they frantically called for the Master to flee. As we got closer they lost all courage and ran for their lives away into the darkness of the garden.

I halted the troop of police with a raised hand, and they waited silently for my identification. The Master's face was calm, and he looked at me expectantly. You had a sword in your hand, Peter, and I know you would have used it to protect the Master's life. Darius's eyes were blank and expressionless. My heart went out to him. Stepping forward, I greeted him as Master, embraced him tenderly and kissed him.

120

Instantly, we were surrounded by the Temple police who dragged Darius roughly from my arms and shackled his wrists with chains. I ordered them to leave the other two men. They had the one they had come for and they did as I commanded. In no time at all, Darius was bound and being marched away. Before following, I glanced quickly at the Master. There was a look of shocked astonishment on his face as he gazed after the disappearing Darius. Guiltily, I turned and ran to catch up with the police and their prisoner.

We were soon in the courtyard before the grand mansion of Caiaphas, where we were ordered to wait as it was still in the small hours of the morning and they were awaiting the arrival of the members of the Sanhedrin who had been summoned for the trial.

The police gathered around a charcoal fire to warm themselves and servants brought out hot spiced wine for them. They drank and made lewd remarks to the serving-maids. I kept apart from them, for even though I was cold I found their company too loathsome to share the heat of their fire.

One of them began to curse Darius for causing them to lose a night's sleep, and the others agreed with him in surly voices. One went to Darius, who was standing quietly by, his head bowed and his wrists still bound, and ordered him to apologise to them. He did not reply, and the man spat contemptuously in his face. The others called him vile names and jeered at his silent meekness. Another one pulled a length of dirty cloth from his tunic and, blindfolding Darius with it, winked at the others, saying the man was a prophet, and knew things that others did not. He spun him around and slapped his face, telling him to prophesy who had struck him. Enjoying the joke, and laughing uproariously, the others formed a circle around Darius, pushing him and spinning him and hitting him. I stepped forward and protested at their behaviour, telling them to stop, but they snarled at me that I might be next if I didn't shut up, being just as much to blame for this missed slumber.

Darius made no sound as he was whirled around like a doll between them, and his passivity seemed to enrage them all the more, for they became like savages, kicking, spitting and fisting him with savage blows, and swearing in the foulest of language. Blood poured from Darius's nose and he spat out a tooth, but still he uttered not a single word.

Eventually the men grew tired of their game and returned to the fire, the chief bully retrieving his blindfold and roughly wiping the blood from Darius's nose and mouth with it. And still he retained his stoical silence. His bravery astounded me, right to the end.

It was then that I saw you, Peter, peering into the courtyard from the street outside. I went to the gatekeeper and told him to admit you, and he did so, asking if you were one of the prisoner's followers, which you denied. Puzzlement was written on your face, but I whispered quickly that we should not be seen together and that I would explain all to you later, which indeed I am doing now, so much later than expected.

You muttered that the Master had returned to the room

at Joseph's house where we had had supper and wanted to see me there. We parted furtively, and you went to join the group around the fire, where I heard you again hotly deny that you had anything to do with their captive.

Then the doors of the house were opened and we were called to enter. Darius, flanked by two guards, was escorted in and led to the centre of a huge hall, around which a ring of High Priests were seated, many of them yawning and peevish for having been called from their beds.

I was met at the door by the priest I had made the bargain with, who handed me a purse of coins, telling me that I could count them if I wished, but all thirty pieces of silver were there. Our business was finished. I could stay or go as I pleased. I decided to stay and watch the proceedings, making myself as inconspicuous as possible by standing in the shadow of a pillar behind the assembled High Priests.

As I had advised him, Darius remained silent to all questions and accusations that were hurled at him. A handful of false witnesses made various statements about his deeds and teaching, claiming that he had set himself up as the Messiah and demanded the worship of the people, but none of them had ever seen him before and could only speak from hearsay, and they often contradicted themselves and each other. One of them claimed that he had said that the Temple should be destroyed, which caused a ripple of angry muttering among the priests, but nothing definite could be proved against him, and a faint hope was beginning to rise in me that they might have to release him through lack of evidence, when the Chief High Priest, Caiaphas, stood up.

A portly figure with a massive beard, he strutted around Darius, glaring at him with his eyebrows knitted in a fierce frown. He asked him why he did not speak. Had he nothing to say to all these accusations? Darius remained silent, his eyes on the floor. Then Caiaphas commanded him to answer this question. Was he Christ, the Son of God?

Slowly, Darius raised his head and stared in Caiaphas's face. Then he spoke. His voice was quiet, but clear. Yes, he said. He was.

Over the gasps of horror and angry oaths Caiaphas's voice boomed in triumph. Blasphemy! What need was there for further witnesses? They had all heard the blasphemy from his own lips. What was their verdict?

In a unanimous chorus of indignation they said that he should die. Many of the priests rose from their seats and surrounded Darius, spitting at him and slapping him. It was announced that he was to be taken before Pontius Pilate, the Roman procurator, to be officially sentenced to death. The doors of the hall were thrown open, and out they all swept in malicious glee, Darius being pushed and pinched and jostled in their midst.

In the lowest of spirits I made my way to the Upper City in the pale light of dawn. If he had only kept silent he might have been saved! And why had he said the one thing that was bound to inflame them the most? It was almost as though he wanted to die.

As I entered the courtyard of Joseph's house I suddenly realised that he had not been present at the trial. In fact many of the Sanhedrin had been absent, it probably having been difficult to summon them all at such short notice. I wondered how Joseph would have reacted, had he been there and seen Darius being tried in place of the Master.

I climbed the steps to the room above the stable and knocked with great trepidation at the door, which was bolted from the inside. Receiving no reply, I put my mouth to a crack and whispered that it was I, Judas. The bolt was lifted and the door swung open. I entered and it was shut and bolted again by the Master. He stared at me stonily and accusingly in the gloom. In an icy voice he asked me to explain myself. I stammered out that it had not been my idea, but Darius's. I had confided in him about the plan and we had both agreed that it would put the Master in mortal danger. It was Darius who had suggested taking his place. I told him how the police had treated him, and said I would rather have died than to submit the Master to such barbarous cruelty.

He covered his face with his hands and called Darius's name in a voice full of despair. Then turning to me fiercely, he said that I had broken my promise. Again I had acted behind his back. After giving my word to do as I was commanded, I had deliberately defied him. I was responsible for the suffering that Darius, whom he loved more than a brother, had endured and would endure. He rued the day he had taken me as a disciple and he would never trust me again.

I begged him to believe that Darius and I had merely contrived to spare him pain and humiliation. I sobbed out the story of the trial and the charge of blasphemy and the taking of Darius to Pilate. Frantically, I held out the purse of money that I had received from the priests, but he stared at it incredulously, backing away as though I were offering him a handful of scorpions.

Flinging open the door, he told me to take it back to them and tell them I had given them the wrong man. I had cheated them. I repented, and they must release him. Darius must be saved at all costs!

Babbling that I would do as he said, and reminding him that there was still the chance of his release at the Passover amnesty, I seized his hand and covered it with kisses, but he snatched it away, wiping it on his tunic as though it were polluted, and told me to go without delay. If Darius were to die, he would hold me alone responsible.

I flew through the street like a maniac, the purse of coins clutched tightly in my hand. Reaching the Temple, I observed no formalities, but charged down the private corridors to the room I had already twice visited, pushing aside those who tried to obstruct me. The startled and indignant faces of the High Priests looked up as I burst into the room. I panted out my message. They had the wrong man. He was innocent. It was not the Master they had condemned. I had misled them. Cheated them. They must release him and I would return the money. I held out the purse with trembling hands.

They looked at me scornfully, one suppressing a bored yawn. He said that it didn't matter. The one I had delivered to them suited their purposes. He had openly claimed to be the Messiah and was therefore guilty of the most heinous crime of blasphemy. The process of the law had been

126

generated and could not be halted. I had earned my reward and I could keep it. My guilty conscience was no concern of theirs.

Disdainfully, they returned to the counting of their gold. In a rage, I opened the purse and flung the silver coins on the marble floor. They bounced and rolled with a cling and a clatter, disturbing them enough for one to click his fingers and summon two guards to my side, who, gripping my arms, forcibly escorted me from the chamber, while I ranted over my shoulder that the man they had was innocent and that they must release him. They threw me out into the sunshine on the Temple steps.

Stumbling to my feet, I made my way down to the Praetorium, where the Passover amnesty was to be announced.

The large courtyard in front of the building was packed with people waiting to petition Pilate. Roman guards stood on the steps, spears in hand, their faces stony and impassive. I pushed my way through the impatient crowd, and when I was nearly at the front the crowd fell silent as Pilate emerged from the palace.

He was followed by Darius, who was flanked by two soldiers. My mouth fell open when I saw him. He was almost unrecognisable.

Branches of thorn twigs had been fashioned into a crown and pressed onto his head, the spikes digging cruelly into his brow. His face was scarlet with the blood that ran down. His eyes and mouth were swollen and bruised, and his nose looked as though it had been broken. A purple cloak had been thrown around his shoulders and stuck to his back with blood, for it was obvious that he had been scourged. He swayed as though drunk, weakened by the savage ordeal he had been through. I felt sick as I looked at him. I pitied him deeply, but I thanked God that it was he and not the Master who stood there.

Pilate raised his hand to silence the curious and excited muttering that had been aroused by the appearance of Darius. He announced that he had questioned this prisoner and could find no charges to bring against him. But since the Sanhedrin had demanded his punishment they could see that it had obviously been carried out. Then he asked: as he had the power to release one prisoner to them on that day, would they not wish it to be this one – the self-styled "King of the Jews"?

At this a great murmuring spread through the crowd and there was a chorus of protest from the front ranks. Standing on tiptoe I could see that it came from a cadre of High Priests who had been at Darius's trial. They demanded that he be crucified. When Pilate asked them why, they shouted that he had made himself out to be the Son of God, and according to Jewish law he should die. And they warned Pilate that he should think of his own position. Anyone who claimed to be a king was anti-Caesar. If he released him, Caesar would not be pleased.

Pilate turned and spoke quietly to Darius. I strained to hear his words, but it was impossible over the growing, impatient hubbub of the crowd. Darius did not answer him, anyway. He seemed not even to be aware of where he was, his eyes blank and lifeless, fixed on nothing. The group of priests continued in chorus to demand his crucifixion.

128

Pilate turned again to the crowd and raised his hand for silence. He asked who they wished to be released.

The courtyard was immediately filled with the sound of raised voices calling the names of those they wanted to be set free, and I added mine to them, shouting the name of the Master as loudly as I could, but my voice was drowned by the majority, who chanted in unison for the release of Barabbas. Hearing no other calls of the Master's name, and realising I was wasting my breath, I turned to the man next to me who was also chanting the name, and asked him who Barabbas was. He broke off to tell me that he was a Zealot who had recently been arrested during an anti-Roman demonstration in the city, a great freedom fighter – far more worthy of reprieve than this pacifist nobody that Pilate was trying to palm them off with. Then he resumed the chant and the whole courtyard echoed with the name of Barabbas. Barabbas! Barabbas! I could hear no other. My heart sank. Darius hadn't a chance.

Pilate raised his hand but the chanting did not desist, rather it increased. At this, Pilate spoke briefly to a guard who marched into the palace and returned shortly with a ruffian of a man who was greeted with wild cheers. He was unshackled by Pilate and, grinning broadly, he bounded down the steps to be mobbed and fêted by the crowd, who carried him shoulder-high out of the courtyard with great jubilation. After washing his hands in a bowl held by a slave, Pilate went back into the Praetorium followed by Darius and his guards.

I approached one of the soldiers on the steps and asked him what would be done with him. He replied that he would be taken outside the city walls to Golgotha and be executed there along with another couple of criminals. Then he told me to be on my way. The prisoner we wanted had been released and I had no more business there.

Sick at heart, I wandered aimlessly through the streets until I came to the square before the Temple, where I sat on a step with my head in my hands, almost oblivious to the cries of the traders and money-changers, and the usual frenetic bustle of Sabbath-eve. Darius was to die, the Master despised me, my life was ruined – but what was that to the world? Life went on.

After a while I pulled myself together and, realising that, however reluctantly, I must take the news to the Master, I rose and made my way to the Upper City with footsteps as heavy as my heart.

It was then that I met you, Peter, coming down the street. We stopped and stared at one another for some time before speaking. I read puzzlement and distrust in your eyes. I don't know what you read in mine. Eventually you asked me where I was going, and I told you that Darius was to be crucified, and I was going to inform the Master. You told me that he already knew.

You, too, instructed by him, had been in the crowded courtyard before the Praetorium and witnessed the release of Barabbas, and hurried back to inform the Master of the fate of Darius. He had become distraught at the news and wept passionately. After recovering himself he had given you several orders, one of which you had already carried out.

You had gone to Joseph and told him that the Master had been condemned to be crucified for blasphemy, and begged him to go to Pilate to ask for his body. Joseph, who at that moment was preparing to leave for an appointment in Capernaum, had been shocked by the news, and promised that he would send servants acting in his name to do as you asked, and lay the corpse in his own private tomb until his return. Expressing deep regret over the loss of the Master, and already mounted, he had set off on his journey, apologising that he could not delay his departure for fear of not arriving before the dawn of Sabbath.

You had also been instructed to forbid any of the scattered disciples that you might come across to attend the crucifixion of "the Master", and you yourself were to return to Galilee to await further orders. You were to reveal to no one the truth of what happened in the garden. And you had promised to do all that he demanded. You added that you did not think that he would be pleased to see me and advised me to think twice before showing my face to him. Utterly dejected, I turned and retraced my steps to the Lower City in your company.

On the way you tried to question me. You did not understand what had happened, you said. Why had Darius been arrested, and why had he pretended to be the Master? The Master himself had failed to enlighten you, and now you were to inform the others that he had been captured and crucified – news which would horrify and dismay them – whereas the truth that he was safe and free would cause them to rejoice. You were deeply confused.

I said that I could not answer your questions then, but

told you to follow the Master's instructions and be patient. All would be revealed in time. That time is now, Peter. I have related the facts to you to the best of my ability, but there is more to follow. My story is almost ended, and soon all will be clear to you.

We parted in the Temple square, shaking hands solemnly like strangers. You searched my eyes questioningly, and then with a deep sigh turned and disappeared into the crowd, on your way back to Galilee. I fought back the impulse to run after you and explain everything. I knew that you would understand and forgive me for what I had done. But it was impossible.

There were also women looking on afar off...
Mark 15:40

... women were there beholding afar off...
Matthew 27:55

... women that followed him from Galilee, stood afar off, beholding these things.
Luke 23:49

I decided to go out to Golgotha and witness the crucifixion. Distasteful though the idea was to me, there was still the chance that Darius might crack under pressure and reveal our secret, although I doubted it. He had proved himself the most stalwart of disciples, and I was sure that he would carry it with him to the grave. I made my way to the East Gate and out into the hilly countryside.

I had not far to go, and climbing a steep escarpment I came in sight of three crosses on which hung their tortured victims. They were naked, and although I was too far away to make out their faces, I could plainly hear their agonised groans. The figure on the middle cross was silent, though he writhed in pain, and I knew that it was Darius.

A group of Roman centurions were seated on the ground before him playing dice, laughing and swearing. How I detested them! I would have given my soul to be able to rush forward and strangle them to death, pull out the nails which pinioned Darius's hands and lift him down from the cross, telling him that his ordeal was over. But there was nothing in the world that I could do but stand there staring in speechless, impotent rage.

Suddenly, I heard the sound of sobbing and, looking down from the cliff on which I stood, I saw two women below me. I recognised them at once as the two Marys – Martha's sister and the Master's mother. The latter was weeping bitterly, and Mary held her in her arms, comforting her.

Not wishing to be seen, I lay down on the cliff edge and peered cautiously over. I guessed that my fleeing brothers must have called at Bethany on the way back to Galilee and given them news of the Master's arrest, and they had come to witness his end. Darius was too far away to be recognised, and they were convinced that his crucified body was that of the Master.

The mother began to beat her breast and accuse herself as she wept. She said that it was all her fault that he had come to such an end. Mary tried to quieten her, telling her that she was talking nonsense, but the mother insisted. He had been brought up to believe that he was special, she said, a Son of God, and she had been responsible.

Mary said that she had heard the rumours of his

conception, but had not dared to question her about them. The mother stopped crying and wiped her eyes. Then, in a tired voice, drained of all emotion, she told Mary her tale, which I relate here without personal comment.

She had been a girl at the time, aged perhaps thirteen or fourteen. She was engaged to be married to Joseph, the village carpenter, a good and pious man. Her father drank, was bad-tempered and occasionally beat her, so she was looking forward to her marriage as a means of escape.

She had to rise early every morning before the family was awake and go to fetch water for their daily needs. One morning she had gone as usual, and found a Roman soldier seated by the well. At first she had been afraid, he being a Roman and a stranger, but he had smiled at her, asked her for a drink, and was charming and handsome. She had tarried, amused by his smattering of her language and the strange utterances he made in his own, and fascinated by the blueness of his eyes.

Suddenly he had caught her in his strong arms in an embrace from which she could not have escaped, and murmuring fond endearments he had carried her to a nearby copse and done things to her which, after her initial fear and pain, had filled her with a mysterious pleasure.

When it was over, and he lay spent by her side, she had realised how late it had become, and fearing the wrath of her father had hastily rearranged her clothing, gathered her pitcher from beside the well, and speedily returned home before the family had risen.

She never saw the soldier again, but fondly remembered his caresses and kisses, until she realised that something was wrong with her body. To her horror and terror, she discovered that she was with child.

Not daring to tell her father, for fear of being beaten to death, she had gone to Joseph and told him the only thing she could think of to save herself. She said that an angel had appeared to her and told her that she was to bear the Son of God.

She being of virtuous and unimpeachable character, Joseph had believed her and hastened the wedding forward, saving her life and reputation. The Master had been born, and when he was old enough to understand Joseph had taken him aside and told him of the angel and the message.

And so he had grown up believing that he was different, destined one day to establish his Father's Kingdom on Earth. Mary had kept silent on the matter, afraid that the truth would turn him against her. But now she wished to God she had confided in him. Even if he had hated her for it, he would have been spared this vile and cruel death.

Mary kissed her and told her that she was wrong to blame herself. His parentage made no difference. The Master was truly a great man and teacher. He had chosen his path and nothing could have deflected him from it. He had been destined to die this way.

In the distance, Darius broke his silence with a long wail of agony. He asked God why he had deserted him. Then he was quiet.

Thick black clouds appeared on the horizon, blotting out the sun and bringing a swirling wind. A storm was on its way.

Another woman appeared and joined the others. It was

Martha. She had been searching the streets of Jerusalem for any remaining disciples, but had found none. All had fled like cowards. Lazarus and his wife were not at home either, having left town to visit relatives in Decapolis. There was no one to help them.

A final cry from Darius was borne on the wind. It sounded ecstatic, almost triumphant. "It is accomplished!" he screamed, and then slumped heavily forward. I knew that he was dead, and I thanked God that his suffering was over.

The Roman guards, irritated by the gusts of sand that stung their bare legs, began preparing to return to the city. Sabbath was about to begin, and, it being forbidden for Jews to be left on crosses over the Holy Day, they took hammers and smashed the legs of the two men on either side of Darius, ignoring their blood-curdling screams. Pulling them down, they left them to crawl away and die. They did not break Darius's legs. He being already dead, it wasn't worth the effort. But one soldier, just to make certain, took his spear and rammed it into his ribcage, causing the women to shriek with horror.

As they were taking down his body, two men arrived and began talking to the soldiers. One showed them something in his hands and the soldiers handed over the corpse to them, which they wrapped in a sheet, picked up and began to carry away. I guessed that they were Joseph's servants and had shown the guards a letter of permission from Pilate for them to collect the body. They were taking it to store in Joseph's private tomb. The women were puzzled, but decided to follow and find out where the body was to be laid.

I, too, followed, keeping enough distance between us to avoid detection, but the women did not look back, intent as they were on keeping the corpse in sight.

The men entered a small garden just outside the city walls. Concealing myself behind a tree, I watched them enter a tomb in the rock cliff, dump the body unceremoniously and emerge wiping their hands on their tunics. After rolling a large stone across the entrance, they went away together, ignoring the women who stood at a distance, silently staring at the tomb.

When they had gone the women agreed together that they would return the day after the Sabbath to reverently wash and anoint the body of the Master. As they left the garden a huge sheet of lightning illuminated the sky, followed by a tremendous crack of thunder and the first tepid drops of a heavy rainfall.

I remained there under the shelter of the trees, staring at the cover-stone. I blessed Darius for the sacrifice he had made and said a silent prayer for his soul. Meanwhile the storm increased its fury, and with each lightning flash and roar of thunder it seemed that God was expressing his anger and outrage at what had been done. It had been horrific. It was a tragedy. But I felt no guilt, for thanks to both Darius and me, it was not the bloody corpse of the Master which lay there in the tomb.

And then suddenly, just as a particularly brilliant flash of lightning whitened the sky, a breathtaking idea came to me, and by the time the deafening crash of thunder had rumbled away, it was clear as crystal. Tears of joy ran down my cheeks, mingling with the rain as I ran out under it, crying and laughing at the same time.

God had given me a plan that would save our seemingly hopelessly lost cause and bring new converts in flocks, droves, millions! I threw wild kisses into the sky as I flew from the garden and into the city, drenched to the skin, but dancing ecstatically in the overflowing gutters.

But Thomas, one of the twelve, called Didymus, was not with them when Jesus came.

The other disciples therefore said unto him, We have seen the Lord. But he said unto them, Except I shall see in his hands the print of the nails, and put my finger into the print of the nails, and thrust my hand into his side, I will not believe.

John 20:24-5

I was soon in Joseph's courtyard in the Upper City, and suddenly my overwhelming excitement dwindled away to a state of extreme nervousness as I mounted the steps to the room above the stable. Again I found the door bolted, and had to pound and call the Master's name before I heard it unlatched, and even then I had to push the door open for myself.

The room was gloomy, lit only by a single lamp. The Master stood before me, his face in shadow. He stared at me in silence, without a trace of emotion, as though I were nothing, and it was dreadful to me. I begged him to speak – abuse me, condemn me – anything but that wordless stare.

And then he did speak. His voice was calm, but as cold as ice. I had murdered his dearest friend, he said. I had destroyed the mission and perverted the prophesies. He preached forgiveness, but never could he find it in his heart to forgive me for what I had done.

If I had not done as I did, I blurted out, he would have been the one crucified. Darius had gone willingly to his death to spare him. He would have been proud to see how bravely he had died! And I reminded him of his own words: "Greater love has no man than to lay down his life for his friend." Darius had done just that, and there would be great jubilation in Heaven at his arrival in place of the Master, who still had so much left to perform in this world!

With a heartfelt groan he turned away from me, burying his face in his hands, and in a tone of the deepest despair said that it should have been him and not Darius. All was finished!

I replied firmly that it was not. In a way it was only the beginning. And as quickly and concisely as possible, I began to relate the plan that had come to me with the flash of lightning in the garden before the tomb.

Darius was dead, and that could not be remedied. The Master, on the other hand, was alive, yet all believed that it was he who had been arrested and perished on the cross. This was the God-given chance to establish himself once and for all as the true Messiah. Removing his hands from his face, he sat down on a bench, saying in a dull voice that he would rather I left him, as my presence and the sound of my voice sickened him. Undaunted, I continued.

He was alive, and none but Peter and I knew it. He had

raised Lazarus from the dead, as there were many witnesses to testify. If he wished, he could now perform the ultimate miracle of his career. He could stage his own resurrection!

He looked at me, comprehension slowly dawning in his eyes. I told him that if he should reveal himself after the Sabbath, whole and well, the conqueror of Death itself, who could refuse to believe that he was truly the anointed One, the Son of God? Even the High Priests and the Romans would be awestruck and afraid. All was not finished. He should seize this opportunity that Darius had given him by his willing self-sacrifice.

After a long silence, the Master reminded me of the body of Darius. It lay in the tomb and could easily be produced as evidence by his enemies. Laughing, I said that that could easily be organised. Due to the storm and the Sabbath, nobody was abroad that night. I would return to the garden, remove the corpse and carry it to the nearby refuse tip where it would soon be disposed of by the wild dogs which scavenged there.

In a horrified voice he asked how I could do such a thing to Darius. Slightly impatient, I pointed out that Darius was dead. He had served his purpose, and his soul was certainly with God. He had no further use for his body. And it had to disappear if the plan were to succeed. I told him of the intention of his mother and the two sisters to anoint the body the day after the Sabbath. The Master should appear to them in the garden outside the empty tomb, and they would be the first witnesses of his return to life. The word would spread that he had risen, was invincible, omnipotent, and it would surely mean the dawning of the Kingdom.

Going down on my knees before him and kissing his hands, I begged forgiveness for the pain I had unwillingly caused him, telling him that all I had done had been for his sake. I was totally devoted to him. My life was nothing without him.

Removing his hands disdainfully from mine, he told me to go about my business. Experience had shown him that once I was set upon a scheme not even he could prevent me from carrying it out. I rose to my feet eagerly and made for the door, promising that I would return to inform him when the deed had been accomplished, but he stopped me, saying that he had a small task for me before I left, and after rummaging among a pile of tools in the corner he turned to me, holding out a heavy mallet and a long, sharp nail.

My mouth fell open in horror. I understood his intention and my blood froze. I exclaimed that it would not be necessary. He looked at me scornfully, and in a voice of granite replied that if we were to convince we must be convincing. He would be brave.

Seating himself on the bench, he placed his right hand palm-upward on the rough wood, offering me the hammer and nail with his left. I backed away in revulsion. I could not do it, I cried. The thought of causing the Master physical pain and scarring his blessed body with my own hands was abhorrent to me.

A look of dark fury swept his face, and he spat out his words. After the long, appalling torture that Darius had endured for his sake, did I think that he was incapable of bearing a couple of paltry wounds? Flinging the implements to the floor, he commanded me to leave. My company revolted him. I had thwarted him all along, acting behind his back and disobeying his orders. Even this last simple request I refused to perform. I was a traitor, a coward, and he detested me.

I could not stand his accusations. They were so unjust and untrue. I reached down for the discarded tools and, taking them up, approached him trembling. The anger left his face, and he looked at me almost lovingly. He told me to strike hard and quickly, and I held the nail over his unflinching palm with the mallet above it, unable to move, as though paralysed. He leaned forward and kissed me gently on the cheek, telling me not to be afraid. Let me show that I loved him enough to follow an order that I loathed to perform.

Summoning up all my strength, I smashed the hammer down on the nail and felt it pass through his hand into the wood beneath. The Master screamed and blood spattered out, wetting my face and shirt. I became hysterical and, sobbing and jabbering, begged him to forgive me for hurting him, but fiercely he demanded that I pull it out swiftly and do the other hand, and I obeyed him, wild with grief at the spilling of his precious blood and his shriek of pain.

The task accomplished, I lay at the Master's feet, weeping and hating myself for what I had done. Gradually, as my sobs subsided, I became aware of the profound silence in the room, and looking up I saw the Master gazing in fascination at the crimson blood that oozed and dripped from his open wounds. As though in a trance, and without raising his eyes, he told me to go and do what I wanted, and never to let him see my face again. He would never forgive

144

me for as long as he lived for handing over Darius instead of him.

Realising the futility of argument, I crawled to the door, broken-hearted. Before letting myself out, I turned to take my last glimpse of the Master. He sat there staring at his bleeding palms and whispering the name of Darius over and over again.

Now when Jesus was risen early the first day of the week, he appeared first to Mary Magdalene, out of whom he had cast seven devils.

And she went and told them that had been with him, as they mourned and wept.

And they, when they had heard that he was alive, and had been seen of her, believed not.

Mark 16:9-11

The storm had not abated, but I was hardly aware of it as I walked through the deserted, rain-lashed streets. My mind had become numb, fixed on the mutilation I had performed on the Master, and my banishment from his company forever.

I made my way out of the city to the garden tomb. There, after a few moments of panic when the stone refused to budge against the pressure of my shoulder, I found a fallen branch and, using it as a lever, slowly managed to move it aside. Entering the tomb, I was struck by the smell and silence of death. I gathered the wrapped corpse stiffly in my arms, dragged it out into the rain and heaved it onto my shoulder. It was cumbersome but surprisingly light, and I staggered out to the city rubbish dumps, the wind whipping and wailing around me.

I laid it in a desolate place where I could hear the howling and barking of wild dogs on the prowl. Stripping off the winding-sheet, I looked down at Darius's pale, blood-caked body lying there in the mud and garbage. Tears came to my eyes, and I asked the forgiveness of his departed soul. I was sure that he would have approved of my plan. Perhaps even, in that flash of lightning, the inspiration had come from him.

Another bolt streaked across the sky and I saw three mangy curs approaching with cunning stealth down the hillside, their eyes gleaming hungrily. I turned and walked quickly away, leaving them to their supper.

I returned to the tomb and replaced the winding-cloth on the slab. I sat there for a while, sheltering from the storm. I pondered the fate of Darius, the rich young man who had given up all his wealth to follow the Master and find eternal life, only to suffer the ignominious death of a criminal and be devoured by dogs among the rubbish.

As for me, I knew that my part in the story was over. Against my will it had been my lot to be cast as the villain, and I would be remembered as such and vilified long after my death, as the Master's name and message spread throughout the land. His life and deeds would be recorded and elaborated upon, and I knew that for the legend of his death and resurrection to grow, I must always be known as the traitor who had sold him for a handful of coins. It had to be so. But I knew in reality I had saved him. And although he hated me for what I had done, I knew that I had done the right thing.

And Darius... he would not – must not – be remembered for the role he had played in saving the Master's life. No one knew of it but you, me, and the Master himself. A wave of panic swept over me, but soon subsided. I was more than positive that you would keep the secret.

I thought of my future. It was necessary for me to disappear completely from the scene for events to proceed. I contemplated suicide, but the idea terrified me. And I had to be certain that the Master would begin the new chapter by revealing himself returned from death with the wounds I had so unwillingly inflicted upon him. If he did not everything would have been in vain, especially the death of Darius.

After a while the storm passed over and the sky became clear. The stars seemed washed, so clearly did they shine, and the wind dropped to a faint breeze. I left the tomb and moved to a part of the garden where I could keep it in view without myself being seen. Lying down on the sodden grass beneath a tree, I fell into an exhausted, dreamless sleep.

I slept throughout the whole of the Sabbath day. There was nothing else to do. Waking occasionally, I remembered where I was and what I had done, and swiftly sought again the blissful oblivion of sleep. The sun dried out my clothes. When night fell I rose and ate some figs and berries from the trees. Then I sat and waited for the dawn. I was utterly and completely alone, but that night I could summon up no emotion, not even self-pity. I was aware only of my breathing, hearing and sight.

The women arrived just as the sun was rising, carrying towels and vessels of water and myrrh. I concealed myself in some bushes and watched and listened. The mother, weary from the journey, put down her pitcher and sank to the ground, asking them to rest a while before opening the tomb. It would require all their strength, and that, along with the grief that they were to spend thereafter, would leave them totally exhausted. Martha sat and put a comforting arm around her. Mary, bidding them rest, said that she would go and see how difficult it was to move the stone, and left them. A few moments later she returned, crying that the tomb was open and empty. Someone had stolen the Master's body!

Martha and the mother rose and, telling Mary to stay and guard the myrrh, they hurried off to inspect the tomb. Mary covered her face with her hands and began to weep in despair.

Suddenly my heart leapt with joy. The Master had emerged from behind a tree and was approaching her. The lower part of his face was covered by a scarf, and his hands were bandaged. He came to her side and asked her why she was crying. She wheeled around and, not recognising him, asked that if he had removed the Master's body she beseeched him to show her where it was so that it could be properly mourned and anointed before burial.

He spoke her name, and with a shock she realised that it was he. Falling to the ground, she stretched out her arms, but he backed away, telling her not to touch him. As she gazed up in astonished rapture, he told her to tell the others that she had seen him. They should return to Galilee, where he would shortly come to them and give further instructions.

He turned to go, but Mary begged him to stay and show himself to his mother. Scrambling to her feet and telling him to wait, she ran towards the tomb calling to the other women. As soon as she had gone the Master walked quickly away and out of the garden.

Mary returned pulling the other two by their hands, but stopped in dismay when she saw that he was gone. She looked around in bewilderment. The Master had been there, she stammered. He had talked to her. She had touched him.

The mother said that she must have imagined it. The shock of finding the tomb empty had been too much for her. Martha tried to put her arm around her, but Mary shook her off, saying that she had not imagined it. The Master was alive! He had risen! Truly risen from the grave! She must go to Galilee and tell the disciples! And singing and laughing, she danced joyfully out of the garden. Martha and the mother looked at each other and sadly shook their heads before following her, the mother reverently clutching the blood-stained sheet which had wrapped the body of Darius.

I remained in the garden for the rest of the day, not knowing what to do. I was overjoyed that the Master had shown himself to Mary, but disappointed that Martha and his mother had not seen him. They believed Mary to have suddenly lost her wits, and so would the disciples if they did not see him in person. I prayed that he would appear to them.

Night came, and I felt totally lost. Where could I go? What could I do? Life without the Master was meaningless to me. Although banished forever from his presence, I had to be somewhere I could at least hear news of his progress.

And so it was that I decided to return to Bethany and throw myself on the mercy of Martha and Mary. They were my oldest friends, and although they might hate me now for what they believed I had done, I knew they would not turn me away. Mary might even welcome me, knowing as she did that the Master was alive.

The village was dark and silent when I arrived. I rapped quietly on the shutter of Martha's bedroom window and she opened it after a while and peered out. She gasped when she saw me, and a look of undisguised disgust came over her face. I begged her to let me in, and she came and opened the courtyard door. I entered quickly and she closed it behind me. Staring at me coldly, she told me to explain myself. I asked how much she already knew.

She told me that a couple of days before, James and John and several of the other brothers had arrived in the early hours of the morning in a state of fearful excitement with the tale that I had led a troop of police to the garden where the Master was sleeping and supervised his arrest. They had fled after delivering the news, fearing that they were being pursued, and saying that the Master was doomed and the mission was over. She, Mary and the mother had set off for the city at once to find out what had happened, but by the time they had got there it was all over.

Enquiring at the Temple, they had learned the place of

execution, the charge of blasphemy, and that it was I who had betrayed him. They had hurried to the place, knowing that there was nothing they could do to save him, and watched helplessly from a distance while the Master had died a horrible and agonising death. They had followed two strangers who had taken the body, and seen where it was laid. Returning again the day after the Sabbath, with the intention of anointing the body, they had found that it had been removed from the tomb. The grief had been too much for Mary and her mind had broken. They had returned to Bethany trying to calm her, but she insisted that the Master was alive and had appeared to her and that she must go to Galilee to tell the men that the Master was coming. She could not be controlled and, to humour her, she had been allowed to set off there that evening, in the company of the mother.

Again she asked me to account for my behaviour. How could I, who had professed to love him so much, have handed the Master over to the authorities for a wretched thirty pieces of silver? I told her that I could not explain. I knelt before her, weeping and begging her forgiveness, and pleading with her to hide me. Disgusted though she was by my treachery, she said that she would give me sanctuary for the sake of the Master, to put into deeds his teaching on forgiveness, even to a miserable traitor like myself. She took me to Lazarus's empty tomb at the end of the garden, and we made arrangements for my daily existence.

That is my story, Peter. It is finished, and I wonder what you will make of it?

Dawn has broken. The little patch of sky visible through the gap is pink and golden with the rising sun. Tonight, when Martha comes with my supper, I will ask her to send for you to come to me. There will be no need for us to converse. I will simply hand you this manuscript, and when you have read it you will tell me whether what I did was right or wrong. I will trust your judgement. You may even be able to petition the Master for me when he returns and bring about a reconciliation between us. No, such a hope is beyond expectation. I must force myself now to lay down my writing and say – it is in your hands.

Your loving brother,

Judas Iscariot.

Fear them not therefore: for there is nothing covered, that shall not be revealed; and hid, that shall not be known.

Matthew 10:26

I am writing again. It helps to pass the time and focus my mind, which otherwise keeps returning to images of the Master's bleeding hands, his harsh accusations and stern, unforgiving face.

I asked Martha last night to send for Peter in Jerusalem. She was surprised and asked why I wanted to see him. I told her that I could not reveal the reason, but I begged her to do it. I asked her merely to say that she urgently wishes to speak to him herself and not to mention my name. When he arrives she should tell him where I am and ask him to go to me. She stared at me suspiciously. Then, with a shrug, she said that she would send a servant to the city the following day.

As she was leaving she noticed my epistle on the slab. She stopped and asked what I had been writing. I said that it was simply some psalms I had memorised in my youth, which I had written down to kill the time. She reached for the pages, asking if she could read them. I snatched them away quickly and clutched them to my breast, stammering that they were nothing. She would not be able to read my handwriting; my spelling was bad; some of the lines I had forgotten and omitted, making the verses unsatisfactory and difficult to understand. She could not read them. They were private.

She looked at me searchingly with a strange expression that made me avert my eyes. I was sweating. I could not let her read the letter. No one must know the truth but Peter and me.

"So be it," she said in a cold voice. If what I had written was so unsuitable for her eyes she would not insist. She left, saying that she would instruct Peter to come and visit her the next evening, leaving me cursing myself for having aroused her curiosity in my document. She will surely inform Peter of it before he comes to see me.

That was last night. Now as I write, I expect his arrival at any moment. What will be his reaction to my testament? Why indeed did I write it? Is it not strange behaviour to invite a guest and then remain silent, presenting him a letter to read?

It was not my initial intention to write to him at all. I desired the writing material to relieve my monotony and despair, but on learning of his return to Jerusalem I developed an overwhelming urge to let him know everything as I remember it, and it is better this way, without having to look into his eyes and answer his puzzled questions, which I would have to do if I related my story verbally. That would be too painful and laborious.

I believe he is coming! Through the gap I can see a lantern swinging through the darkness towards me from the far end of the garden! My throat is dry and my heart is beating fast with excitement. I must stop now and greet him. When he has finished reading I am certain that he will understand and forgive me.

I can't understand. I don't believe it. It is only an hour or so since I saw the approaching light of the lantern. Certain that it was Peter, I stopped my writing and waited for him to enter the tomb. Nobody entered. Instead, the stone before the entrance began to move, and before I knew what was happening it had ground to a halt and I was sealed inside. I ran and tried to push it back, but there are no finger-holds and it is impossible to budge. I have tried and tried. My fingernails are broken and bleeding and I am exhausted. It is a joke. It must be a joke. I will wait and laugh with Peter when he moves the stone aside again soon.

The flame in the lamp is beginning to die and it is becoming difficult to breathe. If it is a joke then it has gone too far. I have tried shouting and screaming but my voice has gone.

Perhaps it wasn't Peter. Martha knows I am here. To-morrow she will come as usual with my supper. She must have told him about the letter. Yes. That must be it. I knew Peter could be trusted. So loyal. So protective! The secret is safe and locked away. Locked away in the tomb.

It is not a joke. The light is nearly gone, a flicker, the bread and wine are gone a long time ago. I cannot endure. Why did he not give me the chance? The light has gone. I write in blackness. Utter. It is finished. Accomplished. Air gone. Forgive me. Master.

And fear not them which kill the body, but are not able to kill the soul...

Matthew 10:28